Naïve. Super

Erlend Loe, born in Trondheim, Norway, in 1969, has appeared on stage and worked in film and video production. He has been a critic for the *Worker's Newspaper*, worked in a psychiatric hospital and been a substitute teacher. *Naïve. Super* is his first novel published in English; he has also written several books for children.

Tor Ketil Solberg, a native of Norway and born in 1971, has been a teacher, photographic reporter and social worker. *Naïve. Super* is his first translated work.

Naïve. Super

Translated from the Norwegian by
Tom Ketil Solberg

Erlend Loe

CANONGATE

This paperback edition published in Great Britain, the USA and Canada in 2005
by Canongate Books Ltd, 14 High Street, Edinburgh EH1 1TE

Distributed in the USA by Publishers Group West and in Canada
by Publishers Group Canada

First published in 1996 by J.W. Cappelens Forlag, Norway

canongate.co.uk

18

British Library Cataloguing-in-Publication Data
A catalogue record for this book is available on
request from the British Library

ISBN 978 1 84195 672 5

Typeset in Joanna by Palimpsest Book Production Ltd,
Falkirk, Stirlingshire

Printed and bound in Great Britain by Clays Ltd, Elcograf S.p.A.

Thanks to my family,
to my little brother Even, and
to Kim, Egil, Kjetil and Alice.

'Anybody who rides a bike
is a friend of mine.'

Gary Fisher

The Wall

I have two friends. A good one and a bad one. And then there's my brother. He might not be quite as friendly as I am, but he's OK.

I am borrowing my brother's flat while he is away. It's a nice flat. My brother has a fair bit of money. God knows what he does for a living. I've been paying little attention to that. He buys or sells something. And now he's away travelling. He told me where he was going. I have it written down. It might have been Africa.

He has given me a fax number, and instructions to fax him mail and messages. It's my little job. A simple and manageable job.

In return I am allowed to stay here.

I appreciate that.

It's just what I need.

A little time to take it easy.

My life has been strange lately. It came to a point where I lost interest in it all.

It was my 25th birthday. A few weeks ago.

My brother and I were having dinner at our parents'. Good food. And cakes. We were chatting about this and that.

Suddenly I surprised myself by reproaching my parents for never having pushed me to do sports at a high level.

It was totally unreasonable.

I said stupid things. That I could have been a pro today. Had a fitness curve. And money. Been travelling all the time.

I accidentally said that it is their fault I never made anything of it and that my life is plain and boring.

I apologised afterwards.

But it went on.

That same evening my brother and I played croquet. It's not something we do often. The old croquet set had rotted away under the garden shed. We drove to several petrol stations to find a new one. My brother paid for it with one of his credit cards. Then we paced out the course and put down the hoops and pegs on our parents' lawn. I chose red and my brother chose yellow. I don't know if they were the colours we used to have when we were younger. I don't remember.

We started playing and it went well for a long while. I quickly got through the first two hoops. Got an extra turn and continued. I was on top of things. I became an attacker long before my brother, and placed my red ball behind a tree and just lay there waiting for him, laughing and making jokes. I became brash.

When my brother started looking towards the bush, things had stopped being funny several minutes before.

I could see what he was thinking.

Surely that's unnecessary, I said.

But I knew he wouldn't care. He placed his right foot on his ball and adjusted his aim to where he figured the stroke would cause the most damage. He stood there for a long time aiming for the edge of the garden. The very end of the garden. Where the grass stops being just grass and becomes more like moss. He made a couple of careful test swings. To make sure he would be able to maximise the power of the stroke, and avoid hitting his own foot, which is the most humiliating thing of all. Then he croqueted my ball into the big bush. He croqueted the red ball really fucking deep into the big bush. Into the heart of the bush. Where the sun never shines.

It was a really fantastic shot. I don't blame him for it. I would without a doubt have done the same thing myself. But my reaction. That is what surprised me.

My plan had all the time been simple and quite cowardly. I was going to casually hang around the finish area, and then croquet his ball so far away that he wouldn't believe it. And if I missed, my back would be free, since he still hadn't completed the course. But if I got him, I would smack him against the peg at many kilometres an hour, and top it all off by saying no when he suggested another game.

I could forget about all of that.

I had missed one time too many. My brother had become an attacker and now my red ball was under the big bush.

I didn't give up. I wanted to come back. I planned to croquet his ball under the car. That was the only thing that kept me going. That he'd pay. That his ball some way or other would get stuck under the car. That I'd be able to watch him crawl on all fours, or on his belly, so that he'd get dirty and start swearing.

But first I had to hit my ball out of the bush. I lifted up the foliage and pushed it aside. Then I shone a torch in there. Back and forth in the heart of the big bush. All the way in there I could see the ball. It wasn't possible to see that it was red, but there was no doubt it was my ball. My brother, naturally, stood laughing.

I took the torch in my mouth and crept into the bush. It was dank, probably just a few degrees above freezing. I have hated this bush for as long as I can remember. Now I was about to strike. I aimed. This would go well. I was convinced it would only be a matter of seconds before I was on top of things again.

I would get my brother, the bastard.

But I took three turns to get out of the bush. And as I stood there brushing off the leaves and earth, still with the torch in my mouth, my brother roqueted me and sent me into the bush once more.

This is one of the reasons why I believe that he possibly, deep down inside, is not quite as friendly as I am. I would not have sent him into the bush twice. Once, yes. But not twice.

When my brother wanted to get me the third time, he missed, and I got him instead. But when I was about to send him under the car, I didn't hit the ball properly and the stroke missed. I must have been over-eager.

From there he made a swift kill. He croqueted me to the peg and the game was over. We stood there arguing for a while. I accused him of cheating and we studied the rule book and argued some more. I said a few things that were really off the mark. In the end my brother asked me if something was wrong. What's the matter with you? he said.

I was going to say *nothing*, but then I felt everything flowing over inside. It was overwhelming and upsetting. I have never felt anything like it, and I was unable to speak. Instead, I sat down on the grass and shook my head. My brother came and sat down next to me. He put his hand on my shoulder. We had never sat like that before. I started to cry. I hadn't cried for years. It must have come as a surprise to my brother. He apologised for having been so brutal during the game.

Everything seemed meaningless to me. All of a sudden.

My own life, the lives of others, of animals and plants, the whole world. It no longer fitted together.

I told my brother. He would never have been able to understand it. He got up and said come on, *shit happens*, it'll be fine. He tried to get me on my feet, boxing me brotherly in the stomach and shouting a little. My brother used to play hockey. He knows about shouting. I told him to take it easy. I said this was serious. My brother sat down and took it easy.

We were talking. I was completely incoherent. Neither of us could understand much of what I was saying. But my brother took me seriously. I'll give him that. I could see he was getting worried. He hadn't seen me like this before.

He said there are probably thousands of people who hit the wall every day. Most of them probably have a hard time of it for a while, but then it gets better. My brother is an optimist. He wanted to help.

I sat there thinking this had to be the pits. I was afraid that I had become fed up with life, that I would never ever feel enthusiasm again.

Then my brother said he was going travelling. He would be leaving in a few days and be gone for two months. He offered to lend me his flat. I said thank you and we sat without saying anything until my brother looked at his watch and realised *Sports Review* had begun. He asked me whether I would object to going inside. It was my birthday after all, and there was cake left.

The next morning I awoke feeling things could not continue the way they had been. I lay there thinking.

It wasn't anything to do with croquet. I was certain about that.

Croquet is a small thing and this was a big thing.

Quite soon it began to dawn on me that this had a direct connection with the fact that I had become 25 and wasn't handling it very well.

To me, growing older has for a long time been associated with a certain uneasiness. I generally don't give a toss about space, but I have a problem with time.

While I was getting dressed I realised there was no way I could spend this day doing the same things I used to spend my days doing.

The days would have to become different.

The nights, too.

I stood for a while looking out of the window.

Then I made a choice.

I cycled up to the university and said I no longer saw myself in a position to complete my degree. The departmental secretary asked me if there was something the matter and if there was anything she could do. I thought her concern was touching, but I didn't feel like talking. I thanked her briefly for her interest, and answered yes to the first question and no to the other.

I cycled back to town and put an end to the rest of my old existence. I visited the paper where I had from time to time submitted material, and told them I wouldn't be writing any more for a while. Maybe never. I also cancelled my bedsit, the telephone and the newspaper subscription. And I sold my books, and the TV set.

The rest of my belongings I fitted into a rucksack and two cardboard boxes. I placed the boxes in my parents' attic and put the rucksack on my back, and cycled home to my brother's place.

There I sat sweating.

I had performed a feat.

No nonsense here.

This was not *Sesame Street*.

The Ball

A few weeks have passed.

I am sitting in my brother's flat.

Once a day I go down to buy some food. And if there is any mail, I open it and fax it to my brother. It is an amazingly long fax number. I feel increasingly sure he is in Africa.

I've been looking for the note on which I wrote down his address, but I can't find it.

Besides this I hardly do anything at all.

I flip through the newspaper or lie on the couch staring into space.

I have no plans.

I still have the feeling that it's all pretty meaningless.

It's no inspiring feeling.

I've turned the tempo all the way down. To zero.

I am thinking that I need to start from scratch. How does one start from scratch?

Yesterday I made a list of what I have and what I don't have.

This is what I have:

– A good bike

– A good friend

- A bad friend
- A brother (in Africa?)
- Parents
- Grandparents
- A large study loan
- A BA degree
- A camera
- A handful of (borrowed) money
- An almost new pair of trainers

This is what I don't have:
- Plans
- Enthusiasm
- A girlfriend
- The sense that things fit together and that everything will be all right in the end
- A winning personality
- A watch

Every time I have looked at the list today, I've noticed that I have more than what I don't have. I have 11 things. I lack 6 things. This ought to be a source of optimism.

But having read the list closely it has become clear to me that it is an altogether unbalanced and bad piece of arithmetic.

It won't even out.

Some of what I have I could easily do without, and several of the things I don't have appear to me as central to living the way I'd like to live.

For example, I'd swap my bad friend for some enthusiasm anytime. Or a girlfriend.

Anytime.

But I know just as well as everybody else that it doesn't work that way.

I played around adding together the numbers on the lists.
11 + 6.

It makes 17. Quite a large number when dealing with essential things in a person's life. For a few seconds I was quite proud. But it makes no sense whatsoever. It's stupid to add together things one has and things one doesn't have. And besides, some of those things are less essential. The watch for example. I wish I had a watch, but I wouldn't claim that it's essential. I just fancy having one. To pay more attention to time. As I've said, I have a problem dealing with time, and I think it's better to confront one's problems than to avoid them. But the watch as essential? Hardly.

It's the same with the trainers. They're not essential either, but I have them. Maybe I could say the watch and the trainers cancel each other out. That makes it 10 + 5. Which is 15. Also quite a big number in this context. But regrettably also useless, and as devoid of meaning as 17.

I must try to think about something else.

I am lying on the couch dozing when I hear a fax coming. I wait for it to come through and for the machine to cut the sheet. It takes about a minute. Now the sheet is falling to the floor. I get up to fetch it.

It's from Kim.

Kim is my good friend. I've known him for a few years. He's a good guy, and in the process of becoming a meteorologist. He is doing his practical on an island up north. As far as I have understood he is alone on the island. He reads a few gauges and calculates something or other. Then he calls the Meteorological Institute at Blindern a couple of times every 24 hours.

I think he is a little lonely up there.

He faxes me all the time. I have trouble keeping up with

his pace. I've told him I'm not capable of faxing him as often as he faxes me. He says it's OK, but I know it weighs heavily on him. Without having said the words, we've kind of reached an agreement where he can fax me as much as he likes, while I only reply when I feel up to it.

It's an agreement I can live with.

I can see from the fax that Kim has been watching some programme or other on TV. He quotes: 1. Quit your job. 2. Go travelling. 3. Make new friends.

I have told Kim how I am doing these days. He's trying to help me. That's good of him. Under my brother's desk I have a box on which I've written Kim. In it, I put all the faxes he sends me. The box is already almost full. After Kim learned that I am staying somewhere with a fax, there's hardly been a quiet moment.

Now I'm lying down on the couch again. Something is going to have to happen. Not necessarily something big. Just something.

I decide to go out and buy something that will make me think about nice things, or preferably just smile.

I visit several shops, but can't find anything that I like.

I try to define some criteria for what I seek.

For some reason I've become caught up in this thing about lists. Lists are a good thing. I'll be making many of them in the time to come. I'm making one now.

After a bit of thinking it becomes apparent that I'm looking for an object which:

- Is small enough for me to carry easily
- Costs no more than a hundred kroner
- Can be used many many times
- Can be used indoors as well as outdoors
- Can be used alone or with someone else

11

– Gets me active

– Makes me forget about time

I sit down on a bench and take a closer look at the list. For a long time. It is an honest list. I am happy with it. Maybe a suitable object exists, and maybe it doesn't. It's not that important. But the list is important. This is a discovery to me. This has value.

I sit there pondering which objects will fulfil my desires. It could be several. But I just want one thing.

Suddenly it is clear to me that what I seek is a ball.

A ball, plain and simple. I feel a sting of eagerness.

It's been a long time since I thought about balls. I'm happy that it came to mind. This is the way to go. Now I just have to find a ball. How does one choose a ball?

The world is full of balls. People use them all the time. For fun, games and probably other things. It all comes down to choosing the right one.

I visit a sports shop.

They have an overwhelming selection of balls. Nice, expensive balls. Made from leather and other durable materials. I examine them, but find them too demanding. I'll be feeling a lot of pressure to perform if I buy a ball like that. The time is not ripe for a quality ball. The element of competition must be downplayed right now. Recreation is the key word. I need a plain, basic ball. And preferably a plastic one.

I go to a toy store. Here the selection is more sensible. Fortunately they only have a handful of models. In a few different sizes and colours. I weigh a few of them in my hand and bounce a couple of them on the floor. In the end I make it simple and choose a red plastic ball of average size. It costs just under fifty kroner.

They give me a bag to carry it in. Then I cycle home.

I fax Kim: In the best of moods. Bought a red ball.

I lie down on the couch with the ball resting on my chest.

Now I'm waiting for evening to come.

When it gets dark I'm going to go down into the court-yard and throw the ball against a wall. I look forward to that.

The Tree

I've been throwing the ball in the courtyard several nights in a row now.

Usually I go down after the late news and place myself in a corner where there are no windows. It is a little-used patch, illuminated only by a single light bulb.

There's something very good about throwing. I don't quite know what it is. More people ought to throw. We ought to be throwing, every one of us. Things would look different then. We would be happier.

I throw the ball against the wall and let it bounce off the ground once before catching it. It's a good ball. It always comes back. And it fits comfortably in my hand. I had forgotten how good it is to feel a ball. To hold it. It's so round. It makes me forget about time.

I'm throwing again now.

The red plastic ball hits the wall and emits a little tone. Then it bounces off the ground and emits another tone. Then I catch it, hold it for a moment and throw it again. I do it automatically. Without thinking about what I'm doing. I can think about other things.

Tonight I'm thinking about my grandfather. A few weeks

ago he told me a story. It's a story about a good world.

My grandparents live in a yellow wooden house they built a long time ago. They have a big garden that they've always spent a lot of time on. Flowers and trees and bushes mean a lot to them. They know all the names and when things are supposed to be planted and when they have to be watered and pruned. They often talk about plants and give flowers to friends and family. It's been that way for as long as I can remember. When they built the house, my grandfather planted an apple tree. At the bottom of the garden. I have never seen that tree. It was gone when I was born. But I've heard about it.

When the tree had grown for many years, it started to yield apples. A lot of apples. My grandmother used to make juice and preserves from the apples.

It was a good apple tree.

But then something happened.

It had been a good summer and the apples were nice and big. They were about to be picked.

But one morning the tree had been destroyed. Several thick branches were lying on the ground. My grandfather said it looked bad. It would not grow apples again. The tree was going to die.

My grandfather went inside to give my grandmother the sad news. Then he took off his work clothes, put on something more appropriate, and went down the lane past the cemetery and down to the college.

There he spoke to the principal.

The college acted, and after some time three young students came forward.

They had been out pinching apples and things had got a little out of control.

They had very guilty consciences.

It was a prank. Not a big thing, but serious enough. And both my grandfather and the principal were concerned with sorting things out fair and square.

A new apple tree cost 150 kroner in those days. It was agreed that the boys should pay for a new tree.

They would pay 50 kroner each.

My grandfather told me it was a lot of money back then.

The boys would pay a weekly sum the rest of that autumn and well into spring, until everything was paid back and they were even.

My grandfather had himself been to that college and he knew the boys didn't have a lot to get by on. They were boarders, some of them were far away from home and their families had already dug deep into their pockets in order to send them to college. They had to take the money for the apple tree out of their own allowances. That probably meant any expensive and boyish activities had to be limited considerably. They could hardly buy anything, not go to the cinema, not treat the girls to a soda, pretty much nothing at all.

Every Saturday the boys came dejectedly to my grandparents' door to pay. They said very little. They just held out their hands and dropped the coins into my grandfather's huge palm. He nodded gravely and confirmed thereby that things were going the way they should. It went on that way. Winter came and went, and then spring.

In May the garden was once again in bloom and the polytechnic was about to go on vacation. The boys were going home for summer. When they came by for the last time, they were all dressed up. It was something of an occasion for them. They rang the doorbell and my grandmother invited them in. She had made coffee and waffles. The boys were served and they made the last payment and shook my grandparents' hands.

The case was closed.

The boys were relieved. They cheered up, and for the first time they talked with my grandparents. They told them about school and summer. They told them where they came from. Their faces were happy. The debt was paid. They were cleansed and could finally hold their heads high.

After a while the boys got up to leave. Goodbyes were said, and they walked towards the door.

Then my grandfather got up.

Hang on, he said, there was one more thing.

And the boys stopped. My grandfather crossed the floor. He went over to the big kitchen dresser and opened it. He stuck his hand deep inside it and came out with three envelopes. Then he walked over to the boys and gave one to each of them.

The boys couldn't quite understand. They looked at each other. Then they opened the envelopes and tears started running down their cheeks.

My grandfather had given them their money back.

I'm still standing here throwing the ball. I've really got into the rhythm of it. I can't see any reason to stop, even though the going is good. This game won't go bad. No matter how long I keep at it, it can't possibly go bad.

My grandfather told me he had been planning to give the money back all the time. It wasn't about the money, he said.

I'm thinking about the boys. They're grown-ups today. Probably over fifty years old. They must have had the feeling that the world was good. That things fitted together. That something meant something.

I wonder what they are doing now. They probably have families themselves, and gardens with apple trees.

My grandfather is a really good guy.

I wonder whether I am a really good guy.

I wonder whether there are any really good guys at all in my generation.

Time

This morning I found a book in my brother's bookcase. It's in English and deals with time and the universe and everything.

I flipped through some pages, but started sweating and had to put it down. It was too much for me.

There are limits to what I can handle right now. I walked around in the flat for a while, feeling uneasy.

To divert my thoughts, I started to look through one of my brother's old photo albums. There are several photographs of me there. I am little. And often dressed in the strangest clothes. Corduroy. Always corduroy.

I must have had outrageous self-confidence as a child.

In one of the photographs I am standing next to my new bike. It's green and has five red ladybirds on the crossbar. I'm wearing a yellow and brown pair of dungarees. I'm going cycling. That was the only plan.

When I awoke in the morning, I would think; the bike. One thought.

Today I wake up and have a lot of thoughts. At least five. It's a hassle.

I don't know what it's all about. What is it about?

I faxed Kim, asking whether his parents used to dress him

up in corduroy when he was little. I also ask him if he knows what it's all about.

He faxes me back answering yes to the first question but no to the second one.

Kim always faxes me back immediately. It's like he's just sitting there waiting for me to fax.

That worries me a bit.

While I sat looking at the sheet from Kim which said yes and no, the uneasiness came back. I realised I had moved, and that I was spending increasingly more time over by the bookcase. The book stood there and I stood a distance from it. I peered at it while moving closer and closer.

In the end I was sitting with it in my lap, thinking I might just as well explore the core of my problem now rather than later.

I'm not quite sure, but I think it was a mature decision.

The book is written by a professor called Paul.

I'm thinking that someone with a name as friendly as that couldn't possibly want to scare me.

I have been reading for several hours now, and I am discovering that my entire being is becoming influenced.

Even though it says Paul is known to write in simple terms about complicated things, I find it difficult.

Paul dabbles with difficult things.

My basis for understanding him is weaker than average.

I opted out of maths and physics after my first year of secondary school. At the time I figured I could see a whole lot of other things I'd rather base my existence on. Today I'm not so sure any more. Maybe it was a mistake.

In other words, I don't understand everything. Maybe I understand even less than I think, but what I do grasp fascinates and scares me.

I had no idea my brother read books like this. There are obviously things I don't understand about my brother.

There's even more I don't understand about time.

In a laboratory in Bonn stands a three-metre-long metal cylinder. Paul writes that it is shaped like a submarine and lies in a steel frame surrounded by wires and measuring instruments. It's an atomic clock, and it is currently the most accurate clock known.

It is more accurate than the earth's rotation.

Such accuracy amazes me. It obviously has little to do with the earth. It's just something somebody has decided. I like that. Strangely enough, I feel time becomes more tangible that way.

I think I'd like to have an atomic clock.

To compensate for the irregularity of the earth, a second is added now and then. The last time they added a second was in June 1994. Nobody ever said anything about that.

The definition of time has changed due to atomic clocks. Before, a second used to be one-86,400th of a day, but now it has become 9,192,631,770 cycles of a caesium atom. I think it's a lot.

This information puts me out of the game. I feel unwell and need to fetch the ball. I throw it for a while against the refrigerator before I'm able to continue reading.

I remember when we used to drink milk in primary school.

Many of us had digital wristwatches. With a chronometer function. We had hundredths. We timed the most absurd things. It was the big thing in those days.

For a long time it was all about drinking your school milk as fast as possible. I always took more than five seconds, but Espen, that thug, drank the entire carton in well under a second.

In light of what I have just read, I think that's amazing. Personally I engage in very little that takes less than a second. On occasion I take photographs with a shutter speed of one thousandth of a second.

But that's nothing compared to what caesium atoms get up to. Can I be sure that it's valid? More than nine billion cycles per second? I can't picture it. It's too many. My ability to estimate how many units there are in an amount is limited. I can easily tell whether there are four or nine cows in a field, but if it's more than fifteen I have to count. And anything more than a thousand doesn't really matter.

I have no means of controlling the caesium atoms.

I have to assume that Paul knows what he's talking about.

I have to take his word for it.

Now I've read some more.

It gets worse and worse.

Paul says gravity influences time.

The man knows no limits.

Totally without warning he says that time is influenced by gravity and by movement. I look at the sleeve of the book. It's from a serious publisher. What he's saying is probably right.

I get annoyed.

Why hasn't anybody told me about this?

Don't physics teachers understand that this kind of information makes all the difference? Are they stupid?

The reason I opted out of physics was because we sat drawing protons and neutrons without grasping how it all really fitted together. I was bored. I'd much rather turn to face the girls and make a ring with my left thumb and index finger, and then move my right index finger in and out of this ring repeatedly.

Time was never mentioned.

Not one of my teachers has ever mentioned time – not so much as a word. I ought to find out whether they know anything or not.

Maybe they've known all along. In that case I ought to wreak revenge. I ought to give them a hard shove in the back when they least expect it.

I feel cheated.

I feel I can't trust anybody any more.

Time on the sun passes one two billionths slower than with us. It has to do with gravity. Paul says gravity is stronger up there.

I thought time was time and gravity was gravity.

Evidently that's not the way it is.

With a couple of really good atomic clocks one could prove it in the Empire State Building.

I'm not making this up.

If one places an atomic clock at the bottom of the Empire State Building and another one at the top, after a while one will see that the one at the top goes faster.

During the course of a human life one would save a few thousandths of a second by staying at street level.

Those sitting at the top would be a little older than the rest of us.

Now I'm putting the book down.

I feel I'm becoming groggy. I'm in rebellion.

There is no time.

I can hardly see the conclusion being any other.

There is at least not any one, single time.

My time. Your time. Paul's time. The sun's time.

Lots of times.

Many times equals no time.

If that's the case I ought to be glad.
Why aren't I glad?
I feel stressed.
Maybe I'll be glad later.

The Bike

I'm still not glad.

I was mad to read that book. Blind courage.

I no longer feel so sure that Paul is just friendly.

It is possible that time does not exist, although things still move. Life is in motion. We are born and we die. I grow older. What good does it do that time is not the same on the sun?

Someone ought to come and employ me. Someone ought to ask me to build something. Carry something really heavy. Sandblast something very big.

It's been a long time since I worked up a real sweat.

I've written a new list. It shows what used to excite me when I was younger. It's quite long.

- Water
- Cars
- Balls
- Telephones
- Animals that were bigger than me
- Fish
- Mirrors
- Bed sheets with sharp creases
- Wood-chipping

- Crossing my fingers when lying
- Riding in elevators
- Lorries
- Sticks
- Animals that were smaller than me
- Loud noises
- Tractors
- Trains
- Aeroplanes
- Policemen
- Fires and firemen
- The tram
- Outer space
- Things that were completely red
- Ants
- Swans
- Dentures
- Paint
- Staplers
- Things that could be thrown
- Saws
- Plasters
- Milk
- Seaweed
- Heights
- The colourant in blueberries
- Lego
- Things that moved faster than other things
- Snow
- Trees
- Knots
- Liquorice snuff

- Rubik's Cube
- Lawnmowers
- Cameras
- Poo and pee
- Pine cones
- Soap bubbles
- Africa
- Things that had a golden or silvery colour
- Strong wind
- Soda
- Things dad did

My existence was full of these things. It was so nice and uncomplicated. When I wasn't sleeping I ran around and was excited. I never walked. I ran.

I look at the list for a while and then fax it to Kim. I feel I owe him a fax now.

I speculate about making a list of things that excite me today. I find pen and paper, but notice that I am hesitating.

I am afraid the list will be a short one.

I should never have stopped running.

Now I'm on my way down to the shop to buy a litre of skimmed milk. When I return, the courtyard is full of children. There's a kindergarten in the courtyard. I hadn't noticed until now.

A boy on a tiny bicycle with side wheels comes over to me. He is wearing dungarees and a cap. And on top of his cap he has a blue bicycle helmet. He looks at me and at the milk I've bought. He asks if I'm the owner of the cool, red bike. I nod in the direction of my bike, which is parked against a wooden fence, and ask him if that's the one he's talking about. It is.

It's mine, I say.

The boy is full of wonder. He says he wants to have a bike like that.

We walk over to my bike to have a look at it. It is big and red. The boy feels the frame. I am wondering how he knew it was my bike.

He's seen me lock it, he says. And he tells me that he lives in the next building. All the way up top.

Then you have a short way to the kindergarten, I say.

He nods.

I've seen you throwing the ball too, he says.

Are you awake that late? I ask him.

Sometimes, the boy says.

I ask him his name and he says it's Børre.

You've also got quite a cool bike, I say.

Børre says it doesn't belong to him.

He says it belongs to the kindergarten.

Børre is quiet for a while. Then he asks me whether I use a helmet.

I feel like lying and saying yes, but stop myself. I say no.

You must, Børre says. And he thinks I should buy a helmet as soon as possible, and preferably today.

He explains how one of the dads in the kindergarten crashed into a car while he was cycling. He didn't have a helmet and had to spend several days in hospital.

You're right, Børre, I say. I'll buy a helmet.

Børre asks me if I'm going cycling now. But I'm not. I'm going upstairs to drink milk. He wants to know if I might be going cycling later. I don't know. Maybe tonight, I tell him.

Børre wants to watch me cycle, but he's not in the kindergarten at night, he says.

Maybe you'll see me from the window, I say.

Maybe, says Børre.

He stands there looking at me as I walk towards the stairs. He waves when I turn around.

Later it strikes me that I should have put Børre on the bike and wheeled him around the courtyard.

He would have liked that.

The Master

Once I played until I fainted.

I had just got slalom skis and was so excited that I forgot to eat. I skied the whole day without eating.

In the end I fainted from exhaustion and crashed into a lamp post. I had concussion, and Dad had to take me to the hospital.

The doctor said that playing all day long was fine, but that I had to remember to eat in between.

I fainted because what I was doing was so much fun that I didn't have time to take a break.

Something about that is incredibly good.

That eagerness.

It's quite far away.

My mood has been varying these last few days.

I am trying to get a picture of my situation, but the pieces won't quite fall into place. I don't really know where I am.

A lot has changed over the last few weeks.

The days have become different. The nights as well.

But I don't feel satisfied. Not yet. There's definitely a handful of essential things missing. I have no idea where to look.

But I have the ball.

Fortunately, I have the ball.

Every night I throw the ball against the wall for quite a long while.

My brother is coming back in a month's time. Then I can't live here any more. I have a month.

I admit I am nervous about how this is going to turn out.

I am trying not to act tough. I could have lit a cigarette and acted as though nothing was going on. Maybe I could have fooled somebody. A couple of girls. Kim. I could possibly have fooled Kim. But sooner or later I would be sitting there again. On the grass, with my brother's or somebody else's arm on my shoulder, crying.

Because there's something the matter. There is clearly something the matter.

What I could really use is an older man. A mentor. One who could tell me how things fit together.

He would have asked me to do chores that I felt were meaningless. I would have been impatient and protested, but done them nontheless. And eventually, after several months of hard labour, I would have realised that there was a deeper meaning behind it all, and that the master had had a cunning plan all the time.

Suddenly I would have been able to see great patterns. See various things for what they are. Draw conclusions about the world and people. I would also have become able to restrain myself and bring out the best in others and all that. And the master would say that he didn't have any more to teach me and then he would have given me something. A grand gift. Maybe a car. And I would have said it's too much, that I couldn't accept it, but he would have insisted and we would have said farewell in a sentimental but sound manner. And then I would have driven out into the world and met someone, preferably a girl, and established a family and maybe a business that could have turned out some good products and services.

That's how it should have been. Damn. It's obvious.

It should never have been different.

But such masters do not grow on trees.

I've never met a single master.

Everything points to me having to take care of myself.

I am trying to think who I look up to.

There aren't many of them.

These I admire:

– Laurie Anderson
– Gandhi
– The Salvation Army
– Carl Barks
– Astrid Lindgren
– Orson Welles
– Olav H. Hauge[1]
– Lars Lillo-Stenberg[2]

I am convinced that it's all about eagerness. That it's missing.

I must find it. Get it back.

It's out there.

It's probably pointless to talk about it.

It's a bit Zen.

I'll never make it as long as I try to.

Only when I don't try, will I make it.

Fucking Buddhists. They think they're so bloody clever.

[1] (1908–94) Lyricist
[2] Contemporary singer-songwriter and lead vocalist of alternative (naïve-) pop band deLillos.

Life

A human being weighing 70 kilograms contains among other things:

- 45 litres of water
- Enough chalk to whiten a chicken pen
- Enough phosphorus for 2,200 matches
- Enough fat to make approximately 70 bars of soap
- Enough iron to make a two-inch nail
- Enough carbon for 9,000 pencil points
- A spoonful of magnesium

I weigh more than 70 kilograms.

And I remember a TV series called *Cosmos*. Carl Sagan would walk around on a set that was meant to look like space, speaking in large numbers. On one of the shows he sat in front of a tank full of all the substances human beings are made of. He stirred the tank with a stick wondering if he would be able to create life.

He didn't succeed.

The Forest

It's spring.

Suddenly it's hot.

Today I found a pair of bicycle shorts in my brother's cupboard. And a T-shirt.

I made myself a packed lunch and filled an old bottle with water. I also took the ball.

Then I cycled out into the forest. I'm in the forest now.

It's completely quiet here. And it's a weekday, so there's nobody else about. They are at work. They are at university.

May they enjoy it.

I have, as I have mentioned, a pretty good bike. It's got many gears. And big knobbly tyres. I cycle anywhere. I'm a hardcore rider.

Before I bought the bike, I read a whole load of brochures and catalogues from many leading bicycle manufacturers. I enjoy looking at pictures of bicycles, imagining what I would look like sitting on them. One of the brochures was by a guy called Gary Fisher. He lives in California. Gary boasts about being the one who invented the mountain bike. Chances are he is right. He has a large, expensive catalogue with pictures of lots of nice bicycles and their technical specifications, and he's had his people put in quotes of things he's said.

There's one place where it says '*Anybody who rides a bike is a friend of mine.*'

I like that.

I feel all those who cycle are my friends. One big family.

When I meet others who are cycling, I sometimes say hi.

But today I am alone in the forest.

That's also nice.

As I was leaving the flat, Børre came over to me. He was asking whether or not I had bought a helmet.

I said I would get one when I had some money.

He reminded me what happened to the unfortunate dad in the kindergarten. I nodded and said I'd be careful.

But I'm not particularly careful.

Riding fast on forest trails is fun.

Sometimes I ramp off roots and rocks.

When I told Børre I was going to the forest, he said his father had seen an elk there once. He was proud.

I have also seen elks, but I didn't have the heart to tell him.

We made an arrangement that I'm going to tell him about all the animals I see. So far I've only seen a horse and a squirrel.

I cycle myself to a sweat, and stop by a pond for a bath.

I'm having a bath even though it's April and the water is cold.

While I lie in the sun drying, I throw the ball up in the air. I'm lying on my back, throwing it up in the air. I'm usually able to catch it, but every now and then it bounces away.

Then I have to get up and fetch it.

Now it's rolled off for the last time.

I can't be bothered to fetch it.
It can lie there until I have finished drying.
I'm thinking about where it went wrong.
It's probably quite fundamental.

My parents have done a decent job. I don't blame them for anything. I've also had good times in school. Nobody was ever mean to me. At least not over a long period of time. Occasionally it happened that someone said something nasty or something, but then I just kicked them on the shin, or punched them in the stomach. No big deal.

It must have been something else.

For some reason I suspect that I know too much about things it's stupid to know a whole lot about.

I know a helluva lot.

This is what I know a lot about:
- Movies
- Literature
- The Media
- Politics
- Celebrities
- Art
- Advertising
- Aerodynamics
- The Information Society
- Roland Barthes
- Computers
- History
- Language
- Music
- Supermodels
- The Sahara

And when I say a lot, I mean a lot.

I know names, dates. Hundreds of them.

I know who was first on Mount Everest.

I know who directs the most unintelligent American sitcoms and soaps.

I know of a survey that shows that in 1957, one year after Brigitte Bardot starred in the movie *Et dieu créa la femme*, 47 percent of all French conversation was about Bardot.

I know that when air hits an aeroplane wing, suction is created on top of the wing, and that is what makes planes fly.

I know what Aristotle thought.

I know what other philosophers have thought about Aristotle.

I know how much Claudia Schiffer earns.

I know that time passes a little slower on the sun.

I know how long Christo and Jeanne Claude spent wrapping the Reichstag in Berlin.

I know the recipe for Coca-Cola.

I know a helluva lot.

I'm not the only one who knows these things.

Many people know more than I do. That's fortunately not my problem.

My problem is what I am supposed to use it for.

What do I do with it?

It's confusing.

I could of course appear on *Jeopardy* and win a trip to Greece. For two. But I don't have a girlfriend. I would have to go alone. And what am I supposed to do in Greece? There is no reason to believe that I would feel any better there.

I am not so stupid that I don't see the use of a certain amount of knowledge. But I don't feel convinced about what is important and what isn't. I lack direction. An overview. How does one get an overview? Maybe it comes with age. But maybe not.

Am I supposed to just go around waiting like any other idiot?

I should never have learned how to read.

The mother of a friend of mine told me that she used to go to some kind of club when she was little. I don't know exactly what it was. It was probably a place where kids played or sang or something like that.

She thought the name of the club was Barnas Sus[3], and she was proud to be part of it.

She thought it was a grand name. When she learned to read, she realised she had been wrong and that the name was Barnas Hus[4]. She was terribly let down.

I feel the same way.

It must have started as early as when I used to watch *Play School*. All the stuff about today's number, and that when the little hand is close to five, the time must be something to do with five. The hostess, well-intentioned and tremendously optimistic though she was, didn't exactly do me any favours. Today I know all the numbers and letters. I read as fast as anything.

What I'd like to know is what I'm supposed to do with it.

It's a little late to talk about this now. Maybe a bit silly.

The damage is done.

I can't pretend that I don't know what I know.

But it's crap. It really is.

Give me a ball.

Give me a bike.

Those are formats I can handle.

On my way home from the forest I see the horse again. It's brown.

[3] Lit. 'The "Buzz" of Children'; connotes a joyous atmosphere of children playing.
[4] 'The House of Children.'

The Animals

As I am locking the bike, Børre comes over to me again.

Kindergarten is over for the day. Now he's playing by himself. He is building a castle in the sand pit, and wants me to help him.

I tell him I am going upstairs to change and have a bite to eat, but that I'll be down afterwards.

Fax from Kim.

It's been a while since I heard from him. He writes that he's been busy. The weather conditions have apparently been quite extraordinary up there. But now it's over. The conditions are dry with a north-easterly breeze. Variable cloud cover.

Kim has spare time.

The list of things that used to excite me when I was younger has inspired him to write his own.

This is Kim's list:

− Detective stories

− Tarzan

− A girl in kindergarten whose name was Jannicke, who had long eyelashes

− Another girl in kindergarten whose name was Vibeke, who also had long eyelashes

- Spying
- Pinching apples
- Lego
- Outer space
- Superman
- Radio plays
- My birthday
- Presents
- Theatre
- Christmas calendars
- A blue pedal car
- Climbing trees in summer
- Building a cabin
- Setting fire to Matchbox cars
- Another girl whose name was also Vibeke, who lived one house away from us, and who was older than me and who taught me how to cycle
- Cycling

I think Kim's list is good.

There are several items there that should also have been on mine, but I feel I can't change it now. And take from Kim. It's a bit uncouth. But cycling and detective stories ought definitely to have been on my list. I don't understand how I could have forgotten them. But everything related to girls was completely out of the question as far as I was concerned. I remained indifferent towards them for a very long time. I had girl friends, but never thought of them as girls, much less about them having long or short eyelashes.

I think the awakening came when I was on the bus once and some guy asked me whether I was a boy or girl.

Idiot.

We both have Lego and Outer space. They're given. But I

don't believe Kim not having been concerned with poo and pee. He's probably just forgotten.

It happens.

Børre is still sitting in the sand pit when I come down. He's humming a song I am unable to identify. He's wearing his bicycle helmet. Maybe he has strict parents. Børre has built several cylindrical houses. He has probably filled the bucket with sand and beaten the sand hard and turned the bucket upside down. You get houses that way.

He is asking if I could build a system of roads and bridges.

Of course I can.

We sit there for a while, building and chatting. It's quite pleasant. Relaxing.

Børre thinks I'm good.

I tell him he's good too.

We're both good.

Then he asks me what animals I saw in the forest.

I tell him I saw a horse and a squirrel.

Only two? Børre says.

He figures it's not a lot. The forest is full of animals.

The conversation revolves more and more around animals.

A small element of competition arises. Who has seen the most animals?

I say I've probably seen more animals than he has, but that it's perfectly natural. After all, I'm 20 years older.

Before he was born, I had already seen tons of animals, I tell him.

He asks if I've seen beaver.

Yes.

Reindeer?

Yes.

Pheasant?

Yes.

Bear?

No.

Børre has seen a bear. In a zoo.

In the zoo, all right, I say. I have also seen bears in a zoo. But I thought we were keeping zoos out of it.

Then, we might just as well include animals we've seen on TV, I tell him.

Børre asks if I've got cable TV.

After we have discussed a little back and forth, Børre agrees to abandon the thing about zoos. We agree to find out what animals we've seen in their natural surroundings.

First I suggest that we should include animals we've seen in real life, but Børre soon fouls me, pointing out that animals in zoos are also in real life.

True.

And to compensate for the age gap, Børre is allowed to include animals his dad has seen. I figure it's fine. I was the one who suggested it. I still feel pretty sure I'll win.

When I ask Børre whether he knows what animals his dad's seen, he just nods. He finds it unthinkable that his dad might have seen animals without telling anyone about it.

We agree only to include one specimen of each species, irrespective of sex or age. We won't, then, write stallion and mare and foal. We keep it simple, and write horse.

I'd rather we drop the animals everybody's seen. Otherwise we'll have to list all kinds of ordinary and boring animals. Dog and cat, for example. And cow.

But Børre doesn't think we ought to differentiate.

An animal is an animal, he reckons. You can't blame the dog for being ordinary.

No, you can't, I say.

Børre and/or his dad have seen these animals.

– Horse
– Snake
– Hen
– Whale

I stop him to ask whether it was he or his dad who saw the whale.

It was his dad.

I ask Børre if he's sure.

He nods and goes on.

– Pig
– Goat
– Swan
– Elk
– Reindeer
– Roebuck
– Deer
– Cod

Wait a minute, I tell him. A cod's not an animal. It's a fish.

So what, says Børre.

I groan and say that then we'll have to include all the other fish as well.

Of course, says Børre.

Was I thinking otherwise?

– Haddock
– Coalfish
– Salmon
– Shark

Come on, I tell him. Now you're kidding. Your dad saw a whale OK, but a shark . . . Hardly anybody has ever seen shark.

But Børre's dad has naturally seen a shark.

Where?

Australia or somewhere like that, Børre says.

I wave my arms. There's not much I can do.

Has he seen kangaroo as well? I ask with a certain sarcasm.

Yes, Børre says.

— Kangaroo

— Eagle

— Turtle

— Hedgehog

— Musk ox

— Crab

— Sheep

— Squirrel

— Otter

— Hamster

— Woodpecker

— Cat

— Owl

— Frog

— Fox

— Hare

— Wood grouse

— Stag

— Badger

— Little birds

I should never have started this. Fortunately it's beginning to slow down now. I am grateful Børre doesn't know the names of all the birds.

— Cow

— Grouse

— Ferret

— Dog

There's silence. A long one. Børre is thinking now. I can see he is a little unsure.

Then he says another word.

– Tiger

Tiger? I ask him.

Børre nods.

I don't believe you, I say.

But it's true, Børre says.

I ask where he saw it.

In Africa, Børre says.

But I've got him now. Everybody knows there are no tigers in Africa. Everybody except Børre.

I tell Børre that he ought to run upstairs and ask his dad if he's seen a tiger. Fair is fair.

Børre walks towards the door. Discouraged. He is doubtful.

After a few minutes he comes back down. He is happy. His dad hasn't been to Africa. He hasn't seen a tiger, but he's seen a polar bear. In Spitsbergen. And Børre shows me a photograph his dad took of the polar bear. It looks dangerous. Faced with a dad like that I can't do much.

I strike tiger from the list.

Why did you say tiger? I ask.

I knew there was something I had forgotten, Børre says.

I think that's quite a good answer. He took a chance. It's a straightforward case. Now I'm adding the last animal to the list.

– Polar bear.

That's it.

Now we're on to animals I have seen.

I go through Børre's and his dad's list. I've seen everything they have, except shark and whale and polar bear and kangaroo and otter. Why on earth haven't I seen otter? But I've seen beaver, besides more fish and birds, but so has Børre's dad, probably, if we start going into detail. I can't be bothered, so I shut up.

Børre and his dad have won.

Børre holds both arms up high.

Out of curiosity I ask him which are the animals Børre has seen. It turns out it's not that many. He has seen horse, cat and dog, cow, fox, cod and coalfish. And some birds, whose names he doesn't know. Eight animals and some birds.

Børre is pleased that I have seen fewer animals than he and his dad. He asks if I want to come up with him and play with the race car track.

It sounds fun, but I'm tired. And besides, I don't feel like meeting the travelled dad.

I tell him I'll think about it. We could maybe do it another time. Børre says we can do it anytime.

Four

Now I'm watching a music video on my brother's TV set. I hardly ever watch TV, but now I'm watching a music video. It's a great video. The woman singing is called Alanis something-orother. She is singing while driving a car. In America. She's got three girlfriends with her. They're on a trip.

Alanis is dressed in a brown jacket and a dark red cap, the one in the passenger seat has a dark red sweater, and the two in the back seat are wearing a green sweater and a yellow sweater.

The song is great. It seems to be about how we have very little control over what's going to happen to us.

The verse is quiet, but the chorus rocks. I sit bumping my back against the chair in sync with the music. Here comes the chorus again.

Suddenly, I discover that all four girls are the same. They're all Alanis. We only see one at a time. She has changed sweaters and become each one of them in turn. She's on a trip with herself. And she meets her own gaze in the rear-view mirror when she sings. It's very charming. It looks like she's really having a good time. The Alanis in the front passenger seat is the cutest one. She's the kind of girl I want. She doesn't worry. She's just having fun. Taking things as they come.

While I'm watching her, I think several thoughts.

The first one is that I ought to go to America and drive a car. It looks so cool. To just drive.

The other one is that I dream about meeting an Alanis-girl and living in a house together with her. It'll be the two of us. Me and her. We go for walks at low tide and turn the rocks over, and we will, after a while, when it's time, have children.

The third thought is that I am a BA and don't know what I'm going to become.

This is a problem for me.

I'd prefer to become someone who can make the world a little better. That would be the best thing. But I don't know if it's possible. I don't know what it takes to make the world better. I feel uncertain that it'd be enough just to smile at everybody I meet.

The next-best thing would be to become someone who doesn't make a difference. Someone who makes the world neither better nor worse. It might not be totally fulfilling, but I think there are many in this category. I wouldn't be alone.

The worst alternative is to become someone who makes the world worse. I am going to try to avoid that. At almost any price. But I don't think it's that simple. Maybe I'll get mixed up with some bad and dishonest people. It can happen to the best of us. And then I'll be stuck. And the world will become a little worse and I'll stop meeting people's gaze on the street.

It can happen, just like that.

The fourth thought is that Alanis most likely has a boyfriend, and that he is probably very cool.

The Board

I am thinking about Ferdinand Finne. The artist. The guy who is pretty old, but who always looks damn good and who seems happy all day long while he stands there painting his pictures of the sea and flowers and whatever.

Someone told me they'd seen a TV interview with him. It was several years ago. He was asked how he would describe his life. If he stopped to look back, what would sort of be the essence? Finne thought about it for a long while, and then he replied that not so long ago he had begun to notice that life, in a way, was a bit like a journey.

I hope it's true. That I've had it told to me correctly. That Ferdinand Finne really said that. It's really wonderful.

I assume Finne knows how to read. That he knows a thing or two about the world. If that is the case, it could mean that things are less complicated than I think.

I hope I'll be able to say the same if someone asks me to summarise my life in sixty years. That I can just mull it over for a while and say that I think life can be compared to a journey. And feel that I'm having that thought for the first time. That I came up with it myself and that I mean it.

So far, I'm absolutely unable to say something like that.

There are too many confusing elements present. Things I know. Thoughts I have. Sarcasm. Things I think I ought to be doing and places I ought to be going. Always other places.

Sometimes I envy the goldfish. Apparently, they only have a few seconds' worth of memory span. It's impossible for them to follow a train of thought. They experience everything for the first time. Every time. As long as they themselves aren't aware of their handicap, life must be one long happy story. A party. Excitement from dawn to dusk.

This is what I would paint if I were a painter.
— Bicycles
— Deserts
— Balls
— Girls
— Clocks
— People who are late for the bus
Now the phone is ringing. I answer it.

It's my bad friend, Kent. I have known for a long while that it would be only a question of time before he found me, and it is with a certain apprehension that I've waited for him to call. He has been in touch with my parents and they've obviously given him my brother's phone number. There's little I can do. He's on the phone. He's wondering why he hasn't heard from me. The truth is, it's always him who calls. Sometimes I think he's not aware that that's the case. Maybe he believes that we phone each other.

Kent works at the Central Statistics Bureau. He knows how many litres of milk Norwegians drink per annum and how often people have sex. On average, that is. And he is a member of Mensa, the club for the two percent (or whatever it is) of the population who have an IQ higher than some number or other around 140.

He loves exercises that are meant to define the intelligence quotient. Patterns that are meant to fit together. Association tests. How many litres of water run through such and such cylinders, and when the trains will meet if the southbound one starts in Bodø and travels at 80 km/h, and the northbound one starts in Lillehammer and travels at 84 km/h, but stops for 27 minutes in Trondheim. Sometimes he brings those kinds of tests to parties.

He keeps trying to convince me to take the Mensa test. He says I am probably not dumber than he is and that I'll pass with flying colours, but I know he hopes that I'll fail. I am never going to try.

Kent is a really bad friend to have. Useless. I have indicated several times that I don't think he's anything much, but he doesn't seem to take it seriously. I've known him since primary school and we have done fun things together, a long time ago. He's not so easy to get rid of. I also feel a bit sorry for him.

Kent's world is full of what I don't want my world to be full of. When he opens his mouth, there are almost invariably stupid or unpleasant things coming out of it. He is a human being living in disharmony with almost everything. What he talks about the most is girls and what he fancies doing with them. He subscribes to the most bizarre forms of sexual practice and seems to have no clear means of separating right from wrong. Things that are demeaning and vulgar to me are fine to Kent. Fortunately, I see him rather seldom, but the sad thing is that he is even less in touch with himself than he is with me.

To me, Kent represents everything I try to get away from. The dark side of man. If Kent had a part in a *Die Hard* movie, he would get crushed by a car or an elevator during the opening titles.

He also talks too loud. And now he is on the phone waiting for me to say something. An evening with Kent is the last thing I need right now. One beer, I tell him. We can have one beer.

While I am tying my shoelaces, a fax comes through from Kim. I am grateful that something is taking my mind off Kent.

Kim has also seen some animals. Not very many. But at least some.

- Dog
- Cat
- Pig
- Pigeon
- Seagull
- Crow
- Sparrow
- Robin
- Titmouse
- Cockerel
- Hen
- Fish
- Crab
- 'O' shell (Kim's drawn a line through this word)
- Horse
- Cow
- Donkey
- Dromedary

It's quite a pathetic list. Kim must have lived a rather static outdoor life. One day I'll take him to where the elks are. I know a place.

When I arrive at the cafe, Kent is sitting there with two guys whom I don't know. Kent tells me one is about to finish his doctorate in physics and the other one is a graduate physician in the process of becoming a psychiatrist. I greet them.

Kent asks me what I am up to, and I tell him that I have left university and started throwing a ball because everything suddenly seemed so meaningless to me.

This is evidently an item of news that Kent is unable to take in properly. He lets it pass and asks whether I've met any girls lately. I tell him I haven't met a single one.

Kent is silent. I sort of start chatting to the two others. The psychiatrist is asking me whether I see my choices as waves breaking. I ask him if it's doubt he's talking about. Whether he means that I'm in doubt when I am faced with choices. He means what he says.

Do I see my choices as waves breaking?

I guess in a way I do. I say yes.

The psychiatrist nods and says that's good. If I didn't, I would have been psychotic.

We toast my not being psychotic.

I tell the physicist that I've been reading a bit in a book about time. I mention a few quick key words: Einstein, the theory of relativity, gravity, that time doesn't exist.

Exists, doesn't exist – what's the difference, he says.

I tell him not to make jokes. I explain that this is important to me.

The physicist says this thing about the theory of relativity is something he hasn't been particularly occupied with. Not beyond what was on his syllabus a few years back. There aren't many people who understand the theory of relativity, he says. But he has heard those that do think it's a beautiful and elegant theory.

I ask him if he understands about time passing slower at the top of the Empire State Building than at the bottom.

He shakes his head. He doesn't understand it, he says. But he doesn't doubt that it's true, and he has learned to accept it. He's learned to live with it. Most of the time he thinks about other things, and he feels I ought to do the same.

Without warning, Kent begins to talk about a girl he has been seeing. It's a dirty story. I listen until it's finished without commenting on it. Afterwards I ask Kent how he's doing at the Central Statistics Bureau. He's quite content and I say fine.

Then I say I'm going home to sleep.

You could always give me a call some time, Kent says.

Sure, I say.

The next morning I wake up early, feeling that I have to buy something that can redress the damage done by my contact with Kent. I feel as though I've taken two steps backwards.

When the toy store opens, I've been standing waiting a good three-quarters of an hour. And I've got my list ready.

I want something that:
– can help me release aggression
– has striking colours
– can be used over and over and over
– makes a noise
– makes me forget about Kent and time

This is a lot to demand of an object in a toy store. It would be a lot to demand of an object in any store. But it might still work. I am taking my time. There are no other customers in the store. The staff follow me intently with their eyes while I walk around among the shelves. I've already told them I don't want any help. I must do this on my own.

The breakthrough comes at the Brio section. There is a toy that I recognise from when I was little. It has the potential to fulfil all the points on the list. It is a Hammer-and-Peg.

The box is nice and red and the board is pictured with a

little boy hammering. The board is yellow and says Brio in large, red lettering. The pegs that you hammer down are yellow and the legs on the board are blue. The hammer is red and green. I feel a good sensation throughout my entire body. I remember the hammer-and-peg as a very satisfying toy.

When all the pegs are knocked flush with the board, a sense of cohesion arises. Things join together. They have meaning. Then you turn the board over and hammer the pegs down again. It is an infinite-action machine that provides its user with a sense of cohesion.

I don't demand more from anything. Neither people nor objects.

If I hammer for a sufficiently long time, I may be able to achieve a sense of meaning on as much a global as a personal plane. Anyway, I have nothing to lose. Now I've bought the hammer-and-peg, and I'm cycling home. Today will be The Day When I Begin to Hammer. Here I go.

Vacuum

The last few days I have hardly done anything but hammer.
I've hammered morning, noon and night. It is an exquisitely
monotonous activity that fills me with pleasure. The thoughts
stop coming. I am full of gratitude towards Brio.

Finally I'm on my way somewhere. I am gaining a certain
extra energy, and I feel stronger. I've even gained courage to
read on in the book about time. Now I'm reading about light.
That it's fast. Almost 300,000 kilometres per second. In a
vacuum. It is a bit slower in the atmosphere. And a metre is
defined as the distance covered by light in the space of one
299,792,458th of a second. In a vacuum.

I fax Kim and ask him about vacuum. Whether it's something he's clued up on. Whether he can explain to me what
it is.

He faxes me back saying that a vacuum is nothing. A void.
Devoid of air, of everything. That's what vacuum is.

I had hoped it would be something more. But I suppose
it's enough. If it's already nothing, there's no reason to say it
in a more complicated way.

The bright side of the fax is that Kim knows how a vacuum
is created. He has done it a few times, on rainy days, he says.

I am to take a jam jar and fill it half-full of water and put it in my brother's microwave with the lid off. And leave it there until the water boils. Then I have to take it out and put the lid on. That's when something will transpire with the pressure inside the jar and I will find myself with a vacuum in my hands. There's nothing to it.

I open the refrigerator and find a jar of blueberry jam with the expiry date less than a month away. I pour the contents in the loo and clean the jar with soap and hot water. Then I fill it half-full of water and put it in the microwave. I set it to Max and let it rip. Now it's boiling.

I remove the glass and wait for a few seconds until the steam has died down. Then I put the lid on. I have created a vacuum.

In a way it's a bit of an anti-climax. There's nothing to look at, really. But I know that everything inside the jar that isn't water is a vacuum. It is, strangely enough, quite a satisfying thought. I wonder what I'll use it for. Light passes through the jar all the time.

I've read that light is particles. Photons. And now they're passing through the jar. Faster than the photons outside the jar.

To add an edge to the proceedings, I take the jar into the bathroom and switch the light off. Then I switch on my bicycle lamp and hold it up to the jar. Silence.

There's nothing to suggest that something in my brother's bathroom is moving at almost 300,000 kilometres per second. It is a totally undramatic situation, but I am still gripped by a kind of momentousness.

My brother's bathroom is smaller than 300,000 kilometres. It's much smaller. I can't figure out what happens to the photons. I don't know whether they stop against the wall or whether they are thrown back. The only thing I know is that they don't disappear. Paul writes that nothing disappears.

We remain there in the bathroom for quite a while. The vacuum, the photons and I. It's gripping.

After a while I switch off the bicycle lamp and leave the bathroom. I put the vacuum jar on the windowsill. It can stand there and let the lucky photons that hit it get a surprise. I feel good. Similar to the feeling I get when I feed the little birds, or give money to someone who has less than I do. Then I sit down with the hammer-and-peg and hammer until the *Evening News*.

The Bird

Here is another story. This one is also about a good world. It took place before I was born.

My brother and my parents were on holiday in Denmark. They had rented a cottage at the beach. I don't know how old my brother was that summer, but I think he was quite young. Maybe seven years old. He just ran around, swam in the sea and threw sticks and other things into the water. He must have been having a good time.

One day he found a bird that had hurt itself. I think it was a baby seagull. It just lay there. It couldn't fly. My brother had no experience of sickness and death. He just felt sorry for the bird. He felt sad about it lying there, sick and all alone. He wanted it to be well again, and fly off to its family and be happy and do the things baby seagulls usually do.

My brother took care of the bird. He carefully carried it home to the cottage and put it in a box lined with cotton. He gave it food and water and talked to it.

The bird was the first thing my brother thought about when he woke up in the morning, and the last thing he thought about before he went to sleep.

In the morning he would run outside and see how the bird

was doing, and at night he would say goodnight to it and gently stroke its wing.

My brother began to love the bird. It became important to him that it would get well. My parents also hoped it would get well. They could see how much feeling my brother was investing in the bird. They were afraid he would be sad if it died.

My brother thought the bird was getting better by the day. He figured he could see it. He kept thinking it would get well anytime, and that it would fly back to freedom. But it didn't turn out that way.

One morning, while my brother was still asleep, Dad found the bird dead. He buried it a distance from the cottage. When my brother awoke, Dad said the bird had got well and had flown away. He said my brother had cared for it so well and been so good to it that it had got well again.

Neither Mum nor Dad had the heart to say that the bird was dead. Maybe they thought my brother would experience painful things soon enough. They wanted to protect him while they could. My brother had done everything in his power to save the bird. And now he was told that it had flown away. He was happy. It was good to think that the bird was out there somewhere. In good health. And that he had helped it. The only thing he felt a little bit bad about was that he didn't get to say goodbye.

My brother must have had a feeling that the world was good. That it was possible to do something, and that things sometimes didn't get worse, but better. My brother still believes the baby seagull got well. Nobody has ever told him what really happened.

The Girl

It's early morning and the doorbell is ringing. I'm putting the hammer-and-peg aside to open the door. Børre is outside, with a man who I guess is the dad. I'm surprised, but I ask them in. The dad introduces himself and we shake hands. I can see Børre has been crying. The dad is a bit ill at ease. He asks me if I'm redecorating the apartment.

I say no and ask him what made him think I was.

He heard someone knocking something, he says.

I tell him the way it is, that I use the occasional spare moment to knock a little. All by myself. Sort of. And I show them the hammer-and-peg. Børre's dad nods. He doesn't quite know what to believe.

The story is that the family are driving to Hamar to visit Børre's sick grandmother, but Børre is refusing to come along. He thinks it is so sad. So now they don't know what to do. Børre has been very difficult. He has been crying for quite a while. That's why his dad came to think of me. Børre has been talking a lot about me. And about my bike.

He knows very well that it's a lot to ask, but still, if I have the time. It would be such a great help. It's kind of a desperate situation. Grandma will be so sorry if they don't come. I ask Børre if he wants to spend time with me.

He nods his head, swallowing.

I say it's perfectly all right. That I didn't have a single plan for the day anyway.

The dad's very grateful. They'll be away overnight, but will return the next day.

I am given the keys to Børre's apartment and instructions for when Børre is supposed to sleep and when he's supposed to eat.

The dad repeats that he is grateful.

I tell him to think nothing of it, and then I ask him what it was like to see a polar bear.

He says it was stupendous. It's an extreme animal. Very big.

Then Børre's mum and dad and little sister leave for Hamar. We go down into the courtyard to wave them off. And now it's Børre and I. We had better come up with something to do. Preferably something fun.

While I have breakfast, Børre is sitting by my brother's desk drawing. He's drawing a racing car. I tell him he may borrow the hammer-and-peg, but Børre would rather draw. He spends a long time on the racing car. In the end he colours it in.

When Børre has finished the drawing, a fax comes through from my brother. Børre thinks it's wonderful. A mystery. He doesn't understand how it's possible. A sheet of text coming straight into the room. He wants to know where it's coming from. I tell him I think it's from Africa.

Børre is asking if he can have the sheet.

I'm just going to read it, then he can have it, I tell him.

I'm reading the fax from my brother now. It sorts out a misunderstanding. It becomes clear that he's not in Africa, but in America. I must have mixed the two continents up. Both of them begin and end with A. And they're both far away. In a way it disappoints me.

Africa is a lot more exotic than America. To have a brother in Africa is exciting. It's a little like having money in the bank. You never know quite how much it has become when you go to withdraw it again. A brother in America is far less spectacular. Everybody has a family member in America at some stage.

I understand my brother has sold something over there. He has made good money and now he wants to ask me a favour. It's something about the dollar being very favourable against the Norwegian krone right now. Very favourable. My brother is asking me to buy a car for him. He will be needing a car the minute he gets home. It would be good if all the formalities concerning purchase and registration have been taken care of. He's asking me to buy a car.

I have to fax him my account number immediately, then he'll transfer enough money to pay for a car. I write my account number on the back of Børre's racing car drawing. I also jot down a few questions regarding the car. What kind of car does he want? What colour? Does he want it to come with an airbag? Then I fax the sheet to America.

A few minutes later the racing car drawing comes back out of the fax machine, in black and white. Børre is ecstatic. Now he's got two racing car drawings in his hand. An original and a second-generation fax copy.

My brother has written; What's this? And where's the account number? across the drawing.

I turn the sheet with the racing car drawing over and fax the account number and the questions again.

My brother replies, saying he'll trust my judgement when it comes to the make of the car. But it has to be a cool car. A status symbol. It must have a fresh and sporty air about it. And the colour must be red or green. Maybe something like olive. And with an airbag.

Børre thinks it's great that I'm going to buy a car. He thinks I ought to buy a racing car.

It is a big assignment my brother's given me. I am flattered. I have never bought a car before.

Børre wants us to fax the racing car drawing to his grandmother. I tell him very few grandmothers have fax machines, but that we'll mail it to her if he's got the address. Børre figures we might just as well leave it if we can't fax.

We go out to look at cars. Børre and I. First we look at the cars in the street. We look through the windows and check how high the speedometers go. To Børre, that's the only thing that matters. He spots a BMW with a speedometer that goes to 280. He thinks I should buy that one.

We go to a Volvo dealership and test-sit a few Volvos. The dealer thinks Børre is my son. He treats me like a potential customer, showing us around and explaining technical things. Telling me Volvo put great emphasis on safety. Børre checks the speedometer. It barely passes 200. He shakes his head.

Børre, I tell him, 200 kilometres per hour is more than you think.

Now we're test-driving the Volvo on the E18. Børre is clapping his hands. He is sitting in a kiddies' seat we've been lent by the dealer.

Are we doing 200 now? he asks.

Almost, I say.

It's a nice car. And green. When I get home I'll fax my brother and tell him it has good road holding, whatever that means.

I come off the motorway and drive back towards town via a country road. It feels good to use the steering wheel a little.

We stop at a shop to buy some ice cream. While we are eating, I read the notices posted by the entrance. Advertisements about bingo and riding lessons. But there's another note. A nice note. Something for Børre. I read it to him.

Hi, my name's Jessica. I am wondering if there's someone who'd like to buy some of this stuff, because I've got some things in my room that I'm not using.

The things are:

- Shampoo, henna, around 10 cm long bottle, price: 10 kroner.
- Body lotion, melon, around 8 cm long bottle, price: 5 kroner.
- Twin trolls with long, white hair and key rings, one has a star on the tummy: 5 kroner for both.
- Stamp kit with packaging and flower: 10 kroner for both.
- White pearl ear studs, unused: 10 kroner.
- Brooch, unused: 5 kroner.
- Power Rangers pictures in a box, around 10 cm long, full of pictures: 20 kroner.
- Piggy bank with Sam the Duck on it: 5 kroner.
- Kinder Surprise figures, 3 lions (2 of the same), a frog, a turtle: all for 10 kroner.
- Cheerfully coloured coil spring. Flexible and pliable. Can walk stairs: 10 kroner.
- An elephant which is a toothpick box of porcelain: 10 kroner.

If you're interested, call and ask Jessica at phone number . . .

Børre is interested. Not in the girlie things, but in the Power Rangers pictures and maybe some of the other things. He doesn't quite know. He has to see the stuff first.

We walk over to a telephone booth to call. It's Børre who is doing the talking. I can hear him ask if Jessica is home. When somebody at the other end of the line wants to know who's asking, Børre says it is he who's calling. Børre.

Jessica and he talk for quite a while. Børre says yes a few

times and Power Rangers a few times. Then he gets the address and hangs up.

The pearl ear studs and the brooch are sold, but none of the other things.

Børre's on fire.

Jessica meets us on the doorstep. She is about twelve and wears her hair in a pigtail. Her parents are also home. And an older sister who looks a little like the one who drove a car and sang in the music video I saw on my brother's TV. She looks my age.

We shake hands with everybody.

Jessica's father is quite taken with the Volvo. He can tell it's the latest model.

Børre and Jessica disappear into Jessica's room.

I get invited for coffee and cookies.

The parents think it's a little embarrassing that Jessica has put the note up in the store. They are worried people might think they are short of money and that Jessica isn't getting an allowance. They explain that it is not the case. They are no worse off than other people, they say.

When Jessica's mother is about to pour me coffee, I have to say I don't drink coffee. She asks me what I'd like instead, and I tell her water or soda is perfectly fine. Or squash. She disappears into the kitchen.

Jessica's father comments that it's unusual not to drink coffee. He is right, of course. I have this discussion every time someone discovers that I don't drink coffee. I explain that I don't disregard the fact that I some day might start drinking coffee, but that I so far haven't taken to it. I have actually never drunk it. I've had coffee in my mouth, but never swallowed. Now Jessica's mother is returning with a glass of orange squash.

Jessica's father is talking about cars. He has a Volvo himself, he says. And there's that thing about Volvo that if you've ever had one, trying other cars is out of the question. He came close to buying a Japanese car once, but abandoned the idea. The car didn't really have anything going for it. Volvo, however. Now there's a car. Safety. It's like a good friend. No nonsense, ever. And he puts down his coffee cup to make a hand gesture that seems to mean: full speed, forever. And sunshiny days.

While he is talking, I sit looking towards Jessica's older sister, Lise. She is looking indulgently at her father. She is pretty.

I tell her father that I agree. Volvo is good. Then I ask Lise what she does for a living.

She's trying to become a photographer, she says. She takes pictures for a couple of women's magazines. But she'd prefer to take her own pictures.

I tell her I also photograph occasionally. I have a camera, I tell her. Nikon.

Nikon's the best, says the father.

Nikon's good, says Lise.

Børre and Jessica are emerging from Jessica's room. Børre is carrying a box of Power Rangers pictures, a bottle of Henna shampoo and a piggy bank shaped like a duck. He's grinning from ear to ear, and asks me for 35 kroner.

When we're about to leave, Jessica's mother asks if we wouldn't like to stay for supper. It won't be long now. I feel it would be going too far, and besides I have to return the car. I decline politely, telling her that we unfortunately have an appointment. We thank them for their hospitality and for the sale, and Jessica and her family wave us off.

As I put the car into second gear, I look at Lise one last time. In the rear-view mirror. It's been a long while since I've looked at a girl and thought that she's the kind I'd like to see more often, maybe as often as every day. But I am thinking it now. She ought to be sitting beside me, in the passenger seat, wearing a red sweater. And we ought to drive here and there. Together. I think everything will be a lot better when I get a girlfriend. It's a terribly immature thought. But I am still likely to hope it might be true. I would in any case not exclude it.

Børre is happy with his day. I have given him a coin that he has deposited into his piggy bank. When I ask him what he is going to do with a bottle of Henna shampoo, he says he is going to give it to his mum. I can see he's looking forward to it.

Outer Space

Børre is sleeping now. He was very tired. We were playing with
his electric racing car track until long after he was supposed
to be in bed. I let him win. And then we played a word game
where you had to say the first word you could think of. Quickly.
I had hoped it would be like I'd say sun, for example, and
Børre summer, but it soon fell apart. Børre kept saying poo.
No matter what I said, he'd say poo. And then he laughed a
lot. But now he's sleeping.

I went over to my brother's flat and sent a fax to America.
I wrote Volvo – full speed, forever. And sunshiny days.

I also fetched a woolly jumper. Now I'm sitting on Børre's
balcony drinking gin and tonic. His parents have a cupboard
full of bottles. When I've drunk myself to courage, I plan to
read on in the scary book about time. Now I'm reading. Paul
writes about Einstein. I understand that Einstein is my friend.

It somehow appears to be integrated in his theory that past,
present and future exist side by side. It's one of the con-
sequences of the theory of relativity. Naturally, I don't grasp
how it's possible, but that doesn't matter. I don't give a shit
about how it's possible. The point is that I feel a little more at
ease after having read it. I refill my glass and continue.

It excites me enormously to read that the experts (whoever they may be) disagree about the nature of time. Some of them want there to be defined, once and for all, a kind of universal time that can function as a measure of change, while others think one should declare the concept of time null and void, as non-existent. We can still have watches. We can keep measuring change in seconds and hours and years, but the idea of time as something which is just there is useless. The latter group has my full sympathy. As far as I am able to, I will lobby for the eventual recognition of their views.

All of this attracts me more and more. My existence is developing some distance from itself. Perspective. Perspective is one of those things one ought to be able to purchase and administer intravenously.

Paul's not afraid of the big thoughts. He writes about eternity now. What's important to know about eternity is that it's not just a very big number, he says.

Eternity is something very different from what is simply vastly, incredibly huge. If the universe has unlimited time at its disposal, it does not simply mean that everything can happen. It means that everything will happen. No matter how improbable it is or how much time it will take, it will happen sooner or later. That means that if I were to live forever, I would do everything and experience everything. Something like that would only be interesting if my brain were able to think an infinite number of thoughts. I honestly don't know if it is.

I put the book down to see if I can think of something. Something new. Anything. I close my eyes and take a few sips of gin and tonic. First I don't think about anything in particular, but then I think about Lise. In a way it is a new thought. It'll do. But there's more. I see pictures. A combine harvester and a beach. And a fish. I don't know whether or not I could call them thoughts, but at least it's all new. I doubt if I'm imaginative enough to live forever.

Now Paul's getting hardcore. He's saying that everything points to the universe having had a precise beginning, and that it will also have an end. Paul says that one day, everything we know will disappear. That's what he's saying.

As a consequence of the Big Bang, the universe is expanding in all directions. The force driving it outward is great, but things indicate that the mass of the universe one day will have a gravity that in total will be more powerful than that force. The movement will then stop, and stars and systems and whatever all of it is, will contract again. Everything will go into reverse, and in the end it'll all simply collapse. Paul calls it the *Big Crunch*.

After that nothing will happen, not a turd. The same way nothing happened before the Big Bang, simply because there was no 'before' in which it could happen. Maybe the universe will start contracting in a hundred billion years, but it could also linger on for a billion billion years. And after that we'll have as many years to pack our bags and prepare for the end.

I love these numbers. Paul's an absolute fiend with numbers. Somewhere in the book he operates with a number he claims will be a one with several million noughts attached to it. It has to do with the distance, in light years, to a celestial phenomenon or a system of something that is located somewhere completely other than our solar system.

He also mentions a prognosis that concludes that the total number of galaxies in the universe seems to be in the region of ten billion, and that each of them has about a hundred billion stars the size of the sun. These numbers are so absurd that I strangely enough find myself in a good mood. It's all so immense. I think Paul feels a bit like this as well. There is so little I can do to make a difference. It is liberating.

My own responsibility is decreasing considerably. I can feel it right now. The sense of responsibility is diminishing. At an enormous rate. I am hardly anything at all. Strictly speaking, that ought to be a frightening thought, but I don't experience it that way. Maybe it's the alcohol playing with me.

This thing about the universe apparently having an end naturally puts a damper on things. Any ideas I might have had about eternal life are sort of getting stuck in the throat. But it doesn't seem to bother me. Not now. On the contrary. I feel more alive than in a long while. Suddenly it feels good to have a deadline to relate to. As a matter of fact, I've always worked well under pressure.

If we are allowed to carry on down here for another few thousand or million years, I'll be happy. Afterwards the universe can explode and collapse as much as it wants.

What's hectic about all this is the thought that I haven't asked to be here. I am just here. So is everybody else. We are all here. But we haven't asked to be. It's not our fault.

Profoundly lyrical, I am sitting gazing out into the night when Børre comes shuffling in. He has woken up because he was having a scary and dangerous dream. He climbs up on my lap and I wrap him in my woolly jumper. I pat him and tell him not to be afraid. It was just a dream. And tomorrow is a new day. Børre rubs his eyes and asks if I can sing a song. Of course I can. I can sing 'Fola Fola Blakken'[5]. It's one of the nicest things I know. When the boy comes smiling into the barn with word from father that Blakken is going to rest, that's when it all fits together. You dream about that, Blakken. Just eat, just stand easy. Maybe wander around the yard, with junior on your neck.

[5] A melancholy song about an ageing horse who is ready for 'retirement'.

I carry Børre back to bed and lie next to him until he falls asleep. Then I go and sit on the balcony again. With a glass of water.

I look out over the town. People are sleeping.

I fill my mouth with water and swallow a little at a time. Water is good. If I had to choose between a lot of things, I'd quite definitely choose water.

I feel better than in a long while. First the ball, then the hammer-and-peg, and now this, all the big numbers. The good feeling of freedom from responsibility. Maybe I'm on my way up. Maybe I'll be all right. And while dawn breaks, I sit there thinking that I'm a really good guy and never mind space and time and all the rest of it.

Crazy Love

I am sitting in front of the TV waiting for the hangover to go away so I can start hammering again. I tried tying a piece of cloth around the hammer, but the sound was still too loud. Brio ought to consider making the pegs out of wood instead of plastic.

It would have suited me perfectly to hammer right now. I could have summed up my thoughts from last night in a careful manner. But now I have to wait.

It's all confusion now. All this stuff about space. I believe I was thinking never mind it all. It doesn't feel that way now. Hubris.

There was no end to how grateful Børre's parents were. They wanted to pay me, but I said I would have nothing of it and besides, I had treated myself to their liquor.

Børre didn't want me to go home to my place. He is a good boy.

TV is a good thing. I ought to watch TV more often. I get pleasantly diverted. I can't quite tell whether the thoughts I'm having are my own or if they're coming from the TV. Animal programmes are the best. David Attenborough explaining that nature is intricate and that it all fits together. Wasps that navigate according to the sun. They know what they're doing, the wasps. They know a lot better than I do.

Now there's a commercial on. I like car commercials. Almost all of them are set in some desert or other. The cars drive fast in the desert. A solitary car under the sun. Volvo's latest commercial is also set in a desert. It looks cool. It's fast. The guy driving has nothing to do but drive around in the desert. He just drives. I think I'll buy a Volvo. A green one. My brother will like it.

Other things that appeal to me are graphic illustrations of how shampoo and toothpaste work. They're so wonderfully educational. I can see how the effective ingredients penetrate the hair or the teeth and cleanse and sort things out. And afterwards it's better than how it was before. That's the point. That things are supposed to get better. But I get aggressive about little animated things and animated food. Crackers that jump out of their box and dance on the kitchen counter while calling the herb cheese in the fridge, and when the herb cheese comes out, the crackers dive into the cheese and spread it all over themselves. It's a strain to watch. Advertising people animate anything these days. Someone ought to shoot them in the foot. There are limits to my toleration of stupidity.

These are things that I think should never be animated in a commercial context:
  — Crackers and bread products
  — Dairy products
  — Chocolate
  — Meats
  — Fish products
  — Cleaners (and dishwashing gloves)
  — Eggs
  — Fruit and vegetables
  — Clocks and watches

I watch Swedish news for a while. They are in the process of wrapping up a case where some council workers have misused council funds. It's quite serious, but it puts me in a good mood. People are completely mad.

In this case a group of council workers have been on a survey in Brussels. Things got a bit out of hand, and they happened to pay for a night of merriment in a sex club with the council's credit card. We're talking more than thirty thousand kroner. In one night. I see the bank statement. That's what puts me in a good mood. It says Dahl's Paint and Hardware, and then it says Texaco a couple of times, and then it says Crazy Love six times in a row.

And those involved have pathetic excuses. One of them says he can't remember a thing from that night. Another claims he never understood it was a sex club. I feel sorry for them.

Dahl's Paint and Hardware
Texaco
Texaco
Crazy Love
Crazy Love
Crazy Love
Crazy Love
Crazy Love
Crazy Love

Now I'm watching a series where we follow the police at work. In America. It's a reconstruction of a good deed two policemen did in Los Angeles a few years ago. I am surprised to find tears coming to my eyes.

I am moved by the reconstruction of the good deed. The two policemen are standing inside the police station telling the story, and at the same time we get to see what happened.

The producers have found two actors who look like the two policemen. It's quite a good illusion.

Here's what happened.

The day before Christmas Eve a black woman sits crying in front of her house in a poor Los Angeles suburb. The policemen come driving past in their police car. They stop, asking her what's the matter. The woman explains that while she was at the hospital visiting her cancer-stricken daughter, someone stole everything she owned. All the furniture, the food in the fridge, even the kids' Christmas presents are gone. And inside the house three kids are sitting feeling sad. There won't be a Christmas this year.

The policemen say there's little they can do. These kinds of burglaries are hardly ever solved. But to be on the safe side they take down what kind of presents she had bought her kids.

When they get back in the police car, the two policemen talk about how this kind of stuff really stinks. Society is going the wrong way, et cetera. They decide to buy presents for the woman's children and pay for them themselves. It's Christmas after all, and they have everything they need, while the poor woman and her children have nothing.

They stop at a toy store and buy what's on the list. A couple of hundred dollars' worth of stuff. They start chatting to the store owner, explaining to him what they're doing. The store owner is touched by the benevolence of the project and says he will pay for half of it. It's Christmas.

When the policemen get back in their car to return to the precinct, there is a call from the station.

They must come immediately.

At the station the boss is asking what's going on, and it turns out the owner of the toy store has called a TV station and that the TV station now wants to interview the two policemen. Happy news stories like this one are hard to come by, and now it's Christmas and people need something good to draw them together. The ball starts rolling.

More TV stations are picking up the story. CNN roll up. Soon the entire United States knows about it. The policemen are congratulated from near and far, and President Reagan calls to say he is proud of them.

People are sending money, and a man offers to give the woman a new house in a better area. Suddenly they realise the woman doesn't know anything about it. She doesn't have a TV, or a radio. She and the kids are probably sitting all alone in that empty house. They think there won't be a Christmas. The policemen decide to wait until the next day, *Christmas Day*.

The following morning the black woman gets up and wakes her children, saying they're going to the hospital to wish the cancer-stricken daughter Merry Christmas. The children feel it's all a bit depressing without presents, but the woman says they have each other and they must be grateful for that.

Sirens. The woman sighs, saying even on this holy day people can't seem to be good to one another. But then the son looks out the window. The street is full of people. Police cars and fire engines and cameras and people. The two policemen are standing outside on the grass, their arms laden with presents. Somebody starts carrying furniture into the house. The woman doesn't understand what's going on, but then she recognises the policemen. They give her a hug and a cheque for eighteen thousand dollars. Then the woman starts to cry. And I cry a little, too.

The headache has passed. I'm hammering.

This business with space again. All the thoughts from last night haven't exactly made me less mortal. When the universe is ephemeral, one can easily feel that human existence is meaningless. Why should I do anything at all?

On the other hand it is tempting to try and make the best of it. I'm here, anyway. The imagination won't cope if I try to picture where I'd otherwise be.

I am not ashamed about having thoughts like these. Maybe I should have had them before. I don't know when people usually think about these kinds of things. Some probably do it as early as age fifteen. I didn't. But I'm thinking about them now. And I'm not ashamed. The whole point of sitting in this flat is just so that I can have these kinds of thoughts. I hope things will get better when I am finished thinking. As a matter of fact there are quite a lot of things I do appreciate.

This is what I appreciate:
– Hammering
– Throwing
– Sitting on the loo
– Sun
– Eating
– Trees
– Friendship
– Beaches
– Girls
– Swans
– Sleeping and dreaming and waking up
– Having someone stroke my back (rare)
– Music (All You Need is Love)
– Children (Børre)
– Water
– Driving a car
– Cycling

If only I had a feeling that things fit together and that

everything will be all right in the end. It would be so good.

Maybe I am spending too much time alone. I ought to spend more time outdoors. Maybe talk to someone. Who would I talk to? Kim is so far away and Kent is a bad friend. I could always chat to my parents, but I don't like worrying them with my problems. I'd rather they believe I am well and getting better all the time.

When I was little, Dad and I used to walk around our house. He would hold my hand and then we'd walk around the house. For some reason I recall it as a very good and meaningful thing. We lived in the house. It was where I ate and slept. And we also walked around it.

I take a break from hammering and cycle up to my parents to tell Dad I'd like to walk around the house with him.

He has just had his afternoon nap and thinks it's a little strange. I tell him not to ask any questions. I tell him I need it. I need to know what it feels like to walk around the house with him. It's part of something I'm working on, I tell him.

Dad puts on wellingtons and a coat, and then we walk around the house. Dad and I. We are walking all the way around the house.

It's not quite like it used to be, but it's all right. I hadn't thought walking around the house with Dad would solve everything. I had moderate expectations. Dad says we can do it again later, if I feel it's necessary. I tell him it's quite possible. Dad also says I ought to go out more. Meet people. Maybe a girl.

Girlfriends

Why don't I have a girlfriend? I can't see any good reason. People not half as friendly as I have girlfriends. Idiots have girlfriends. I absolutely ought to have a girlfriend.

There is a lot of injustice and idiocy in the world. I guess that's part of my problem.

Is it that unintelligent people are responsible for all the silly music and the idiotic books, magazines, films and all the animated foods in the TV commercials?

Could it be that simple? Sometimes I think it is. It is a very plausible explanatory model. Quite attractive.

Or is it that these people are not really stupid, that they mean well, but fail over and over again? That's also a possibility. There's a big difference between being stupid and just being unfortunate. One sure thing is the fact that they have girlfriends. Every single one of them. But not me.

The Pope

I let myself into my brother's flat and discover that Kim has faxed me an extremely long fax. It's probably thirty metres long. It says the same thing almost a hundred times.

Be not afraid.

Kim has loop-faxed it. This is something he's been talking about. He has dreamt about doing it for a long time. It's apparently quite simple.

You put the sheet into the fax machine the regular way and punch in the recipient's number, and while the sheet goes through, you tape the two ends of the sheet together. That way the machine keeps sending the same message until it is stopped, or until the recipient runs out of paper. My entire roll of paper is spent. The expensive roll of thermal paper. It's lying on the floor. All of it. It's a sorry sight.

Kim writes that he found the quote on the back of a book the Pope published a couple of years ago. The previous meteorologist must have left it behind. A Catholic meteorologist.

Be not afraid.

It's a good quote. I'll give him that, the Pope. But not a hundred times over.

I stick the end of Kim's fax into my brother's machine and

start sending the Pope's quote back to him. Kim will be getting a taste of his own medicine. It takes more than an hour to send it all.

Meanwhile, I read a bit more in Paul's book. He actually mentions the Pope. Paul writes that the Pope is fond of the Big Bang theory. The Pope claims to see the hand of God in all of it. He thinks the theory is definitely compatible with the idea of a Creation. God was behind the Big Bang. It's ingenious. The Pope must have been happy when he came up with it. It'll be exciting to hear what he has to say when it all starts to contract. Maybe he'll fall silent.

I tear off a piece of the fax and hang the quote over my bed. It could be good to look at when I wake up in the morning. Catholic or not. Tomorrow I'm going to buy a Volvo.

Elevator

I'm on my way to the Volvo shop, but I've cycled an alternative route taking me past a big, multi-storey hotel. Now I'm standing in the elevator. I am riding up and down. I've been standing here almost three-quarters of an hour. Every time I come down I press the top button, and when I get up top I press the bottom one. People are coming on and going off all the time, but no-one comments on my standing here.

Once in a while when I was younger, we would cycle over to some apartment blocks after school. We used to call them the tower blocks. All the naughty kids lived there. Those who had brothers who were older than us and who went to Sweden every Friday to buy firecrackers and wet-snuff and beer. Everyone who lived in the tower blocks had seen porn movies before they reached school age.

There were wild stories about some of the older brothers projecting porn movies in Super-8 format onto the wall next to the mailboxes. Movies where two ladies would spill champagne over a man so that he had to take all his clothes off. Be that as it may. But these blocks had great elevators.

We went there to ride the elevators. It was a high-risk activity. For some reason they didn't allow us to ride elevators.

We weren't allowed. It was completely unreasonable. Nobody should deprive children of riding in elevators. But all the old ladies would scream and shout and call the police and the janitor would come and chase us. We got a kick every time.

Elevators are brilliant. I'm going to stand here a little longer. The good thing about riding in an elevator as a grown-up is that nobody questions my being in the elevator. Nobody suspects me of just riding the elevator. I look like I'm one of the others.

Now a young woman is entering the elevator. She's going down. I stand there looking at her.

I ask her if she's got a boyfriend.

She replies in English that she doesn't understand.

I ask her in English. *Do you have a boyfriend?*

Yes, she says.

I ask whether he's friendly and does kind things, or if he's not so friendly and does idiotic things.

The woman replies that the world is more complex than I think, but that to be honest, she must admit that she's had boyfriends who have both been friendlier and done fewer idiotic things than the one she has now.

She asks me if I have a girlfriend.

I tell her *no, I don't.*

She nods to herself. She seems to feel a bit sorry for me.

When the elevator reaches the lobby, I exit and get on my bike. I'm cycling away from the hotel now.

Paul

Still on my way to the Volvo shop, I cycle past the university. I sit down on a bench and look at all the students. They're zooming past. My days have definitely become different. But in no way do I feel in a position to gloat.

One day when I have more time, I'll pop by the admin office and suggest that everybody who signs up for the philosophy foundation course be issued a hammer-and-peg along with their syllabus. An agreement between Brio and the university would be beneficial to both parties. Brio would gain valuable publicity, and the university would see a generation of students with perspective and an ear to the ground. In the long run, the entire nation would benefit.

I walk in and sit down in a room where there are lots of computers at the students' disposal. My password (Vann[6]) still works, and I get on the Internet. I think it is overestimated. It consists largely of information I am better off without. It gives me the sense that many people are in a position similar to mine. That they know a helluva lot, but don't quite know what to do with it. Nor are they certain

---

[6] 'Water'

about the difference between what is wrong and what is right.

I've found frightening amounts of worthless information in there. For instance, I think I was a little happier before I knew all the organisations of which Norway is a member. Not a lot happier. But a little. Enough so that it matters.

You try.

Norway is a member of the following organisations: AfDb, AsDB, Australia Group, BIS, CBSS, CCC, CE, CERN, COCOM, CSCE, EBRD, ECE, EFTA, ESA, FAO, GATT, IADB, IAEA, IBRD, ICAO, ICC, ICFTU, IDA, IEA, IFAD, IFC, ILO, IMF, IMO, INMARSAT, INTELSAT, INTERPOL, IOC, IOM, ISO, ITU, LORCS, MTCR, NACC, NAM (guest), NATO, NC, NEA, NIB, NSG, OECD, PCA, UN, UNAVEM II, UNCTAD, UNESCO, UNHCR, UNIDO, UNIFIL, UNIKOM, UNMOGIP, UNOSOM, UNPROFOR, UNTSO, UPU, WHO, WIPO, WMO, ZC.

It's really tiring. Nobody can make me believe that this could be worth knowing, except possibly in a quiz context (at the Ministry of Foreign Affairs Christmas Gala). Never otherwise.

Somehow, knowing that Norway is a member of the Australia Group is stealing my thoughts. I have enough trouble with useful information, never mind being burdened with what is useless.

But many seem fascinated by the fact that this information exists not where we do, but somewhere else. A place that is not here, but everywhere and at the same time always somewhere else. And none of us can be there. Not with our bodies.

It's a bit exciting to think about. I'll agree with that. But it's not damned fascinating. And I look forward to when people will stop saying that it is.

There are two good things about the net.

The first good thing is that one can be surprised, the same way one can be surprised by a newspaper article or a product in a shop, and then one's day changes a little and one becomes glad.

For example, I was glad when I came across a psychology student asking this question: *From a Lego modelling perspective, what is happiness? How would you describe the feelings that you experience through your involvement in Lego modelling? In your opinion, is there a difference between these 'happiness' feelings and pleasure? Does your involvement in Lego modelling help you to attain long term happiness and well as short term happiness?*

The other good thing is that one can easily make contact with people all over the world. That's why I have come here today. I want to try to contact Paul. I want to ask him something. All professors can be contacted electronically nowadays. I feel certain Paul is out there somewhere. I'm doing a search with his name now, and his e-mail address is appearing on my screen. It only takes a few seconds. I've got him now. This is what I'm writing:

Prof. Paul Davies

I am a young man and I don't feel so good. I have a good friend and a bad friend, and I have a brother who is less sympathetic than me. I don't have a girlfriend.

I used to be a student, but I quit. Most days I just sit in my brother's apartment and think, and in the evenings I throw a ball against a wall and catch it when it comes back. And I have a toy that is a hammer and some plastic pegs that go through a wooden plank, and I knock the pegs down and turn the plank around and knock them down again.

Sometimes I read a book that you have written. It is the one about time. I don't like to think about the time that passes, and you seem to say that time doesn't exist and that makes me glad, but I do not feel certain that I understand you perfectly.

You also say that the universe will collapse one day.

You say so many frightening things.

I would love to have the feeling that everything has a meaning and that it will be o.k. in the end.

Right now I don't have this feeling at all.

I would like to ask you twelve questions, and I will be immensely grateful if you answer.

Here are the questions:

1.   Does time exist?

2.   Does the size of the universe scare you?

3.   Do you sometimes feel that everything you do is futile because the sun will be burnt out in five billion years?

4.   Do you like to throw a ball against a wall and catch it again? Do you do it often? Would you do it more often if you had the time?

5.   If Einstein was alive today, do you think he would have been your friend?

6.   How is it possible that the past, the present and the future all exist at the same time?

7.   Do you sometimes wish you didn't know all the things you do, and were free to run on a beach, careless and ignorant of everything?

8.   Do you think the Big Bang was a coincidence?

9. I did not ask to be born. Neither did anyone else. The size and complexity of the universe makes me feel so small and free of responsibility. It makes me feel that the only meaningful thing to do is to try and have a good time. Do you understand that feeling? Do you have it yourself?

10. Do you think that the human brain is capable of thinking an infinite number of thoughts?

11. Do you disapprove of television commercials that feature animated food, for instance biscuits that dance and jump into the cheese?

12. Do you sometimes start to laugh because the numbers you are dealing with are so huge?

Thank you very much.

When I have finished writing, I press 'send' and the computer sends my letter, straight to Australia.

If I were a professor and knew a lot about time and the universe, I would write thorough replies to everyone asking me about something. All professors should do that. I hope Paul is like me. I hope he replies. I need answers.

Before I cycle on, I do something quite cheeky.

I go up to the Meteorological Institute and tell the secretary I've come for a roll of fax paper for Kim. She knows very well who Kim is and doesn't ask me any unpleasant questions. She just asks how Kim is doing. I tell her that he's very well indeed. Then I get the roll. Simple.

The Rain

Now I'm standing in the Volvo shop. I've been to the bank, and I've got almost two hundred thousand kroner in my pocket. I've never had that before. The dealer recognises me. I'm telling him I'm quite certain I'll be buying the green Volvo, but that I'd prefer it if I could test drive it some more. The dealer says I can test drive as much as I want. I have a hidden agenda.

I drive to the shop where Børre and I had ice cream. The note from Jessica is still on the wall, and I take down the telephone number. Then I drive back to the Volvo shop and say that the car satisfies all my expectations and that I want to buy it. The dealer starts messing around with forms, asking me whether or not I've organised financing. He wants to see bank guarantees, et cetera. I tell him I'd like to pay in cash, and start pulling thousand-kroner notes out of my pocket. The dealer thinks that's perfectly all right. He shows me into the back room and we fill in some other forms. I ask him about registration, that my brother would like to have it done before he comes home, and the dealer calls a mate down at the traffic department. They chat for a bit and it becomes clear that the car can be registered as early as today. Camaraderie.

I comment that the dealer looks happy and ask him if it's

because I'm paying in cash, and he says yes. It is only when paying cash that you're really talking about a purchase, he says. He thinks all the cards and financing systems have alienated people from the original experience of buying. Cash in the hand, now that's buying.

I don't share his opinion, but I think it's good that it is making him happy.

He says I can drive with test plates over to the traffic department. There, his mate will meet me, and everything will be sorted out.

Before we part, I ask him if he knows in which desert the latest Volvo commercial was shot. He doesn't know. The Sahara, maybe.

Now the Volvo is parked in the street outside the flat. I've faxed my brother a brochure about it, plus the invoice. My brother has become a car owner.

I myself sit gazing at Jessica's telephone number. It is also Lise's telephone number. I want to call Lise and ask her if she'd like to meet me.

I am sweating. But I feel I have to call. I must do something. It's time I did something. There are limits to how long I can sit indoors hammering.

They're strange things, girls. One can't avoid them. They're so pretty. And they're everywhere. They always make like nothing. I like their voices. I also like it when they laugh and smile. And when they walk. They're also a bit scary. Sometimes I think they know something I don't. But they're pretty. And hard to get. It never ceases to amaze me that even the friendliest girls become attracted to the most rotten boys. My only chance is to not pretend.

When I was younger, every youth programme on TV and the radio was about being yourself. About daring to be yourself.

Actually, some programmes were about having a place to hang out. But the rest of them were about being yourself. It's only now that I am starting to get a sense of what that means. Whether or not Lise knows, I don't know. It's worth a try.

The likelihood that Lise has a boyfriend is considerable, of course. Why shouldn't Lise have a boyfriend? She's both pretty and friendly and becoming a photographer. She probably has a boyfriend. Now I'm calling her anyway.

It's the father who answers. I introduce myself, saying thanks for the hospitality the other day. He asks me how the Volvo is doing. I ask if I can talk to Lise. He says Lise doesn't live there. She was only visiting the day Børre and I were there. Lise lives in town. And she has a phone. I take down the number. The father has to repeat the last two digits: 31.

I pace the room in a circle. Breathing deeply in and out. This is a small-scale hell. I hammer a little before I dial the number. It rings a few times. Then she picks up the receiver.

Now I'm talking to Lise.

When we've finished talking, I lie on the couch, smiling. It's exactly as though it just stopped raining. Like it's been raining and raining, but that it has finally stopped. And everything smells fragrant and the trees are all kinds of green.

There's something very strange about girls. First they're not there and everything is a little difficult. But then they're there, and things become nicer. It happens incredibly fast. It only takes a few seconds before everything is nicer.

I'm meeting Lise in an hour. I'm quite nervous. I want to have a shower now.

Kiss

New day. I'm waking up now. I've been sleeping for a long time. Lise doesn't have a boyfriend. I drink a glass of water while I think about that.

She was glad that I called. We went to a cafe. First we had Cokes, but then we started drinking beer. And we talked about a lot of things.

I said Lise looks a little like the Alanis sitting in the passenger seat wearing a red sweater. But I said Lise is even prettier. She enjoyed hearing that. She wanted to look like Alanis, but she also wanted to be even prettier. It was a compliment that hit the spot.

Lise has a good voice. I just want her to talk and talk. And she's got a cute little gap between two of her front teeth, and hair that's neither long nor short. She told me what she likes doing.

She enjoys swimming and going for walks in the woods. She likes fruit, and she enjoys photographing people who aren't aware that they're being photographed.

She thought Børre was my son. Of course she did. I told her I don't have a son. And no daughter, either. Not even a girlfriend.

I said I was tired of pretending things are different from the way they are. I said I didn't think we ought to sit and nod at each other and say that we think such and such literature is exciting, or that such and such a film is an important film. We can talk about that later, I said. I told it just the way it is.

I figured, should she think I'm an idiot, better if she did so now, sooner rather than later. She didn't think I was an idiot. I'm quite sure about that. She asked if I was always this earnest, and I replied that it was my first time. She also asked if I was desperate. I said no. I said that for once, I wanted to get it straight.

Then I told her about the ball and the hammer-and-peg and Paul. That's when she began to see what I was talking about. She also used to have a hammer-and-peg as a child, but she couldn't remember whether it was a Brio one. I made her write a list. On a napkin.

This is what used to excite Lise when she was little:
— Creating little worlds in my box under the bed
— Karlsson på taket[7]
— Building a house
— Playing surviving-a-disaster games
— Office, having a filing system
— Shop
— Sneaking
— Chasing on bikes
— Collecting bottle tops
— Blueberries
— Dressing up (as a princess)
— Golden shoes
— Plastic diamonds

[7] Classic children's TV series written by Swedish author Astrid Lindgren.

- Miniature things
- Scented erasers
- Mum's make-up
- Making little cities of Lego in the sand

When the cafe closed, we walked through the Royal Park. I went home with her and we drank a cup of tea. She showed me her camera. And some of the pictures. Large colour pictures.

When I left, she gave me a hug which, in retrospect, I think may have come extremely close to being a kiss. It was probably a hug. But it might have been a kiss.

Scary

Today I've received three faxes. The first two I don't have a problem with, but the third one is scary. If I'm not careful, I'll stand a chance of losing what little foothold I've gained.

The first one is from Kim.

He's seen a badger. He wanted me to know. He has drawn a picture of it, and he says it was something between a large cat and a small dog. His supervisor was visiting him up there. They were sitting outside late at night drinking wine, and it was she, the supervisor, who had seen the badger first. But Kim saw it as well. He seems proud to have seen a new animal. I am happy for him.

The other fax is also from Kim.

He's written a list of things that make him happy. I don't remember whether or not I faxed him my list. Maybe he's done this completely by himself. Nothing could be better.

This is what makes Kim happy:
- Water
- Skyscrapers
- Meeting girls I'm in love with accidentally on the street, when they don't have anything in particular to do that day and me neither

- Swimming
- Cycling
- Free jazz
- Spring
- When girls I'm in love with phone me all of a sudden
- Mornings
- Some books
- Chocolate
- Dark chocolate, maybe with nuts, almonds
- Cognac
- Documentaries made in the 50s and 60s, filmed with a hand-held camera, on grainy black/white film
- Flying/travelling
- When things are completely the way I thought they would be, if what I thought was something good
- When good things happen that I never in my wildest dreams would have imagined
- Seeing a badger
- Getting a fax
- Getting a lot of faxes
- Friends
- Work
- Clouds (sometimes)
- Cat
- Managing what I've wanted to for a long time
- Showering
- Jumping
- Running
- Singing
- Eating
- Sleeping

The list is such a long and appealing one. I'm a little envious.

Kim has a better grasp on life than I do. But I'm getting there. One day I'll be there as well.

The third fax is very disconcerting. It's from my brother. He is thanking me for having bought the Volvo. He wants to do something in return. Something for something. My brother's decent that way. But what he is suggesting is making me nervous. He is offering to buy me a trip to New York. For a week. He's already there, and he says we can live in an apartment owned by some friends of his. In Manhattan. I want to avoid making a decision about the contents of this particular fax. I take the ball and go down into the courtyard. I'm throwing now.

Perspective

I had pictured spending the last couple of weeks before my brother came home taking it easy. Hammering and summarising my situation. Cementing that little trace of security that I had after all managed to construct. But then this fax came and ruined the whole plan. I had almost become calm. I had attained a kind of peacefulness. I can only dream about that now. New York. It sounds scary. Overwhelming. I am afraid of being overwhelmed right now. That city seems too big for me.

There are many reasons why I shouldn't go. Lise is one of them. I am meeting her later today. And maybe other days. I don't know what New York is like, but I can hardly imagine that it would be better than Lise.

I also feel I am in the process of getting a grip on things. If I go, I might jeopardise that. It is unnecessary to seek more confusion than what I already have. Besides, I'm expecting a reply from Paul. I'm sure he'll reply soon. And then I'll know a lot of things. I'd rather know those things than go to New York. In a few minutes my brother's going to call. I don't look forward to that. I have to say no.

Now he's calling.

He insists I come to New York. It surprises me that he is

insisting. I have never heard my brother insist before. We can have fun, he says. And according to him, many things indicate that I would benefit from some exposure. Getting out into the world. I tell him it's really not a good time. I say no, but my brother thinks a no is out of the question.

For once I mustn't think a single thought, he says. Just buy the ticket and get on the plane. He says he'll be giving me pocket money as well. In addition to the trip. It's actually quite a generous offer. But all the people, the noise. I'm nervous.

I ask him if he couldn't give me something else. Maybe a watch. A Rolex. I do want a watch.

Never, my brother says. He says a Rolex costs fifty thousand, and that he wouldn't have agreed to buy one even if it cost a thousand.

The point is, he wants to give me the opportunity to get away.

Things happen when you travel, he says.

What things? I ask.

Perspective, my brother says. And he tells me I mustn't be afraid. He'll be there. My own brother. He's going to take care of me.

Perspective? I say.

The Arm

Lise is wearing a red sweater. We're sitting on the grass, drinking mineral water and eating baguettes with chicken salad. It's almost sunny. I'm saying it's strange when you meet someone. That it's a new planet.

I am saying that I tend to dream my way into relationships. It happens by itself, in no time at all. Suddenly I've thought it all out. I picture her in all possible situations, I picture the house we could be living in and the places we could be going on holiday. And this is happening without me even having talked to her. It could happen while I'm walking down the street and meet the eyes of a girl passing by.

Lise asks me whether I've been thinking like this about our relationship. First I hesitate a little and say no, but it is very clearly untrue, so I say yes.

Lise smiles and says she didn't think I had any plans. I tell her there's a difference between plans and dreams. When I ask her if it bothers her, she shakes her head and gives me a little hug.

I tell her my brother has invited me to New York. Lise is excited. She thinks I ought to go. I say that I had already thought about spending less time sitting at home, and instead going out more and meeting people, but that this was a bit sudden.

I am afraid of being overwhelmed. Lise reassures me. She has a theory about New York. She says there are two things that can happen there, and that it's up to me to decide which.

The first possibility is that I put aside all reservations and take it all in. Like a child. The other option is to keep a distance and pay attention to the little things, try to find recognisable features. Organise and compare.

The first option can lead to becoming overwhelmed. The other one could lead to observations, contemplation and fun. According to Lise. Besides, she thinks becoming overwhelmed can have its advantages. I ask her what she means by that. She thinks that with time, it can provide some perspective.

Perspective? I say.

Now Lise is touching my arm and telling me again that she thinks I ought to go. I like it when she touches my arm. I'd almost consider going just to let her know I appreciate being touched.

She says she can't see why I shouldn't be able to continue hammering and throwing the ball when I get back. I should allow myself this opportunity to get away for a while. Maybe I'll see things differently afterwards. It sounds so right the way she says it.

Form

Now my brother's calling to insist some more. He says sun, he says Central Park, he says good things to eat and drink, he says Empire State Building.

Sights, I say with contempt. What would I want with sights?

My brother says the important thing is not the city itself, but that the two of us are together. Brothers should sometimes be together and do nice things, he says.

I think that's a good attitude to have. But New York is probably far too big.

Isn't New York far too big?

My brother thinks it's suitably big.

I ask him if he is overwhelmed.

He says no.

I ask him if he has ever been overwhelmed or if he's afraid of becoming so.

He says no again.

I ask him if we couldn't rather drive across America in a car.

No.

I ask him if I can bring Lise.

He asks who Lise is and I explain.

He says no.

I ask if I can have a Rolex.

No.

Then I ask my brother what he believes in.

Come on, he says.

What do you believe in, I say.

What do you mean? he says.

What do I mean? I'm asking you what you believe in, I say.

In life? my brother asks.

What else? I say.

You're not kidding? he says.

No, I say.

He thinks about it.

I believe in market forces, he says.

Those free ones? I ask.

Yes.

What kind of thing is that to believe in? I say. That's just crap. Who needs market forces?

My brother says it isn't crap.

Whatever.

What else does he believe in?

He believes in friendship.

Good.

He believes in love.

Honestly? I ask.

What? my brother asks.

That you believe in love, I say.

Of course it's true.

I tell him I didn't think he did.

He asks whether it makes a difference.

I say yes.

I ask whether New York is mostly content or mostly form.

My brother says form, he says I'd have to create the content myself.

I ask him why he thinks I would benefit from going.

He says new places, new thoughts, perspective.

You're sure about this perspective thing? I say.

Positive.

There is a moment's silence.

Then my brother asks whether I give up.

Yes, I tell him. I give up now.

Have a safe flight, he says.

Thank you, I say.

X-Ray

I'm going to America.

I'm going to let it rip.

I stand for a long while looking at the hammer-and-peg.

Maybe it's cowardly of me to take it.

But New York is probably not the most hammer-conducive place in the world.

People who live there probably have completely different ways of releasing tensions.

Why should I hammer and make a fool of myself in New York?

On the other hand, I don't want to pretend I'm any tougher than I am. That could easily cause harm.

I weigh the board in my hand.

It weighs next to nothing.

I don't have to use it. It'll be a support just to have it in the rucksack. To know it's there.

And should I feel the need to hammer, I'll have it right there with me.

I could also go without the hammer-and-peg, and just buy one if things get tight. But that's risky.

I don't know how big Brio are in America. Maybe they

don't have hammer-and-pegs there. In which case I risk bottling up plenty emotions.

I'd be fooling no-one but myself by leaving it at home.

The hammer-and-peg has to come.

If the city is as big as I think it is, I'll very likely need to let off steam.

Besides, it'll look good in the X-ray machine at the airport. I grant the customs people the experience.

Now I'm packing.

Underwear. Socks. T-shirts. Tooth brush. Pair of shorts.

Camera.

Hammer-and-peg.

Meaning

The airport shuttle is leaving in a little while. Lise and I are lying on the grass in the Royal Park. We're eating pancakes that Lise has made. I'm asking Lise if she thinks it'll all be fine in the end. That depends what I mean by the end, she says. If I mean the very end, it's not likely that it will be fine. It is naturally a question of faith, Lise says. Some think they'll be living several lifetimes or that they'll go somewhere good after death. If what I mean is eventually, in a while, that things will straighten out with time, the likelihood is greater. It also depends what I mean by fine.

She asks me where I'm trying to go with this.

I tell her I don't know. I tell her that, what I probably want to know, is whether things will sort themselves out. I don't want all that much. But I want to be fine. I want to live a simple life with many good moments and a lot of fun.

Lise believes that it ought definitely to be within my reach. I say there's not much that can be fun as long as I don't feel existence has meaning.

Can't you just not worry about meaning? Lise asks.

I tell her no. I can't.

What about friendship, Lise says. Us, for example, isn't there meaning in us?

Yes, I say.

There you go, she says.

As the airport shuttle arrives, I take a picture of Lise with her instant camera. I ask her if she'll wait for me.

She laughs and kisses me, and says I must send her some postcards.

I ask her if one a day will be too much, but she doesn't think so. But she'd like me to write them in fun places. Preferably on top of high buildings.

I wave goodbye to Lise from the back seat of the bus. Just when I lose sight of her, her face starts to appear on the Polaroid picture. Now I can still see her after all.

Manifesto

From the airport I phone my parents to say I'm going travelling. When Mum hears I'm going to America, she limits herself to saying that it sounds exciting. Have a good trip, she says.

Dad goes a bit further. He says that if I give him about an hour, he'll have time to write a manifesto for me to hand out on the street when I get to New York. It'll be a manifesto where he denounces everything America stands for, their stupidity, their sick dreams, their foreign policy, and cultural imperialism. Just a small A4 sheet of paper. He suspects most Americans have no idea about the way in which he and other European intellectuals perceive America.

Dad wants to give them something to think about. A lesson.

I tell him my plane is leaving in fifteen minutes. We'll have to do the manifesto next time.

N

I'm on the plane now. I am on my way out into the world. I'm watching a movie that is so bad I feel sorry for everybody involved, and I am thinking about the airline employee whose job it is to select the in-flight movies. I wonder if he is just unlucky, or if he's stupid, and whether or not he has a girl-friend.

In the window seat to my left sits a German lady who keeps handing me cartons of juice. The next time she offers me one, I'm going to say no thank you.

I'm reading in Paul's book again. I like it a little more now that I've written to him. I feel we've established a close relation-ship. That we are in mutual confidence. Paul and I. Maybe he's writing me a reply this very moment. Maybe he's telling me not to worry and that everything will be fine.

He writes that the earth floats freely in space. It rotates and moves. Very fast. We use the sun to keep track of how much the earth rotates. Somebody has decided that the time is twelve o'clock at midday everywhere on earth. Therefore, the time is different in many other places from what it is in Norway. The earth is divided into 24 time zones. We pretend the time is the same everywhere within these zones. If we didn't, we'd have to set our watches four minutes forward if we travelled a hundred kilometres east. That means the time at my parents' cabin would always be four minutes more than the time at home.

As I read, it strikes me that the time in New York is not the same as the time in Norway. It's six hours less. In a way I earn six hours by going to New York. It's a satisfying thought. I'll try to spend those hours doing something pleasant. On the other hand, I lose about one three-billionth of a second every hour I spend at an altitude of ten thousand metres. The trip takes eight hours. I will lose one twenty-four-billionth of a second. It's not a lot. I allow myself to ignore it.

Now the German lady is asking if I'd like another carton of juice. I say no thanks and put my hand to my stomach to show her I'm neither hungry nor thirsty. She puts the carton of juice on the floor and puts one of those masks over her eyes to make it dark. She's going to try to sleep.

I get up to go to the lavatory. There's an Italian queuing in front of me. I've noticed him earlier. He is here with two friends. They're all dressed in suits and they keep walking back and forth. I feel they are up to something fishy. That they don't wish me well.

I am not afraid of flying. At least not the technical side of it. But I'm frightened of people. They get up to so much funny business.

There's something suspicious about these Italians. I fear they're planning a hijacking. The way they smile at each other is ominous. It's a bit like they share a gruesome secret. I know there exists a kind of explosive that can't be traced by metal detectors. For all I know they could have their pockets full of explosives. And they most probably have some unreasonable demand. I feel convinced that if they're going to harm a passenger to show that they're serious, they will choose me. It would be typical. Maybe they'll throw me out over the Atlantic. I feel like asking the stewardess to sing me a song, but don't dare to. I restrain myself and ask for a gin and tonic.

Now Paul writes that the earth is an atypical place in the universe. Most other places find themselves in a dismal vacuum or encapsulated in gases. And the temperatures are often absurd. We couldn't have lived a whole lot of other places.

Maybe we couldn't have lived in many other times either, he writes. It's a very hard train of thought to follow. I am trying to understand it. About ten percent of all the people who have ever lived on earth are alive now. We know that. If we assume that human beings will continue to exist, for thousands or millions of years, that means those of us living now are special, because we are alive at an early stage. Those who come after us will be more typical, because, in a relative sense, it'll be more common to live then than it is to live now. But we have no reason to believe those of us living now are special. And if we're typical, that means few will live after us, and that humankind thereby is approaching the end of its existence.

Paul makes a thought experiment which is interesting, but which makes me sweat. He's asking me to picture two urns containing names written on pieces of paper. In the first urn there are ten pieces of paper and in the other one, a thousand. And my name is on one piece of paper and one only. Where do I think the piece of paper with my name on it is most likely to be? Naturally, that's impossible to know. One can really only guess, but as far as probability goes, the chance is fifty times greater that my name will be in the urn with a thousand pieces of paper in it, Paul writes.

Next, the pieces of paper are removed from the urns, and on the third piece of paper in the urn holding ten, is my name.

The fact that my name is drawn this early is more probable in an urn with ten pieces of paper than in an urn with a thousand pieces of paper.

If this is made to count for everybody who will ever live, Paul claims to be able to calculate that there is a 2/3 chance the total number is limited and that we're approaching the end. Paul admits these are just speculations, but I still feel an incredibly urgent need to hammer.

The hammer-and-peg is in the compartment above me. It's very close, but all my fellow passengers seem to be sleeping. I don't dare to. The Italians are sleeping, too. Or pretending to.

Now it's getting worse. Paul is starting to draw in biological factors. It borders on the unbearable. He says the human being exists due to an unknown number of improbable coincidences that have occurred through history. The larger the number of improbabilities, the nearer we are to the end. If the number is just one or two, humankind's total cycle of existence will correspond quite accurately to the life span of the sun. But if the number is higher, and most biologists believe it is, our remaining time on earth is far shorter.

We can make a formula, based on basic probability calculus, to calculate how long we can expect to survive. If an n amount of improbable steps were involved in the development of homo sapiens of today, and the total life of the sun is eight billion years, we can expect to be eradicated, in one way or another, in eight thousand years.

I hope my brother will be there to meet me at the airport when we touch down. I don't want to be alone.

The City

I think everything is the Empire State Building. I've been thinking that way all day. But my brother says we haven't seen it
yet. I'm thinking it again now.

This is New York. I'm letting myself be overwhelmed. It is
strange being here. I've been hearing about this city and seeing
it on film for as long as I can remember. Now I feel sure for
the first time that it exists. Everybody has arrived here.
Norwegians have arrived here. Poor. With dreams. You can
make it here. Anyone can make it here. Still. I could also make
it here. Make money.

Americans seem to live according to the simple theory that
two is better than one, three is better than two, etc. For example,
they believe two hundred dollars is better than one hundred.
It's a cute theory.

Now I think I'm seeing the Empire State Building again.
My brother is shaking his head. I'm absorbing an incredible
amount of impressions as we walk in these streets. How many
impressions can I handle in one day?

The sensory impulses are queuing up. Some of them will
naturally pass me by. The brain just can't keep up with the
eyes. Or the ears. Or the nose. But I seem to be ranking some

of the impressions as more valuable than others. I have no idea how this classification happens. But it's happening.

I have decided to make a note of the essentials. What is left after sifting it all out. What I remember when night comes and I am about to go to sleep.

I think I'm more concerned with things that are very big and things that are very small than with all the stuff in between. This becomes apparent after only a few hours in New York. Most things are very big here. The houses, for example. The skyscrapers. They're everywhere. And they're big. I have a suspicion that it is partly about prestige. First, one guy built a house that was fairly tall, then his friend built one that was taller. And then everybody went hey guys, let's build some goddamn houses, and let's make them tall. Never mind what's in them, let's build them tall. Let's build them fucking tall.

There is every reason to believe the theory which says that two is better than one also says that big is better than small and that tall is better than short. It is, in many ways, a charming thought.

Hardly any of the houses reveal anything about what's inside. It could be anything. It probably is, too. I've had the feeling several times during the course of today that the houses aren't being used for anything. That they're just standing there.

My brother is reading out of a guide book that there are one million offices in this part of town. He says there are offices in all the buildings I believe aren't being used for anything. I tell him he can't be sure.

The cars are big. The trucks are enormous. They look like they've been designed to kill people.

Many of the people are also big. Fat. Their trainers are all squashed on one side and worn thin because they weigh so much.

117

This is what I so far think is big and long and tall:
- The houses
- The cars
- The trucks
- The fat people
- The pizza slices
- The streets
- The fish lying outside the fish shops
- The avocado pears
- The neon lights
- The park
- Some of the dogs
- The cups from which my brother drinks coffee in cafes
- Some of the shops
- The mailboxes

This is what I think is small:
- The parking spaces
- Some of the dogs
- Some of the bananas
- The chocolate bars
- The plastic spoon that came with the ice cream cone I bought

I am tired, but don't want to sleep. I'm spending my six hours walking around in the streets with my brother. It's intense. I'm beyond tired, and things keep happening all the time. It's a bit like having a temperature. The sounds are getting distorted.

My brother and I have had a trying debate. At first, everything was fine. He came to meet me at the airport and we gave each other a hug. We put my luggage in his apartment and talked for a while. My brother was wondering how I was doing. I told him about my thoughts and worries and about my little activities. The only thing he wanted to hear about was Lise.

He thought the rest of it was rubbish. And he has said he doesn't want to hear a word about time zones, or about time intervals shorter than a second or longer than a light year. And not about space. I may think whatever I want, but I am to keep it to myself. I think he is extremely harsh. He's saying that he had a suspicion I was thinking about things like that. The point of inviting me to New York was to get my thoughts going in other directions.

We're gonna have fun, he says.

I don't doubt that he means well, but I think he's going too far. He doesn't want to hear a word about the hammer-and-peg, for instance. Not one. He's going to break it if he finds me hammering. I'll have to hammer on the sly. It's humiliating. After all, I am an adult. Adults shouldn't have to be closet-hammerers. I am trying to confront my problems in a mature way, but my brother is keeping me from it.

I think he's got problems with time himself, but that he still hasn't found out. One day he'll be the one who hits the wall. When that happens I'll let him hammer as much as he likes. Then he'll have a guilty conscience about refusing to let me do it.

Now I think I'm seeing the Empire State Building again.

The Dog

We are staying in a house where there is a doorman and an elevator attendant. And the apartment is great. But there is a dog in it. There's a dog in the apartment. Someone called David is supposed to come and fetch the dog. He was supposed to come yesterday. I know nothing about dogs. And my brother is afraid of it. It bothers us that this dog is in the apartment. It's a black dog. I've given it food and water, but I don't know how often it's supposed to eat. And somebody will have to walk it soon. It hasn't been outside since yesterday, when the owners of the apartment went to New Orleans to listen to jazz or something like that. It is obvious that the dog wants to get out. It stays over by the door. My brother says I must walk it. He doesn't dare to. I don't even know the dog's name.

I attach a leash to the black dog and go outside. On the way down I ask the elevator attendant if he knows anything about dogs, but he shakes his head and says there's probably not much to know. The dog probably knows where it wants to go.

Now I'm walking on the street in New York City with a dog. It drags me a few blocks to the south, to a park. It wants to smell everything and it pees a bit here and a bit there. It pees on anything.

I've never quite understood about dogs. People say they're so wise. That they have intuition and warn you about things that are about to happen. They alert you to avalanches and accidents. It could very well be true. But this dog doesn't seem particularly bright. So far it hasn't alerted me to anything. In the park the dog goes completely mad. It sees some other dogs and starts jumping up and down. It seems completely irrational.

I distinguish myself from the other dog owners. I don't know what the dog expects of me. I feel everybody is looking at me. A woman comes over to me. She also has a dog. She tells me that my dog and her dog are best friends. I tell her I come from another country and that this is the first time I have walked a dog. I tell her I don't even know what the dog's name is.

The lady says the dog's name is Obi and that I must be firm with it.

Easy, Obi, I say.

I ask how often it's supposed to eat and drink and what I'm supposed to do if it starts to crap. The lady gives me a little bag. She asks me if I didn't get any instructions and I tell her someone called David is going to come and fetch the dog. He could be here any time now.

I speak English to Obi.

Come on, I say. *Good dog.*

Now Obi's sitting down to take a shit. On the grass. I think it's disgusting. Joggers and children look towards me while I pick the dog turd up with the bag. Now I'm standing with a bag full of dog turd in my hand. It's absurd.

This is a completely different life. People must think I'm a dog owner in New York. That I live here and have an apartment and a dog. That I pick up dog turds like this one every day, before and after work. It's a staggering thought.

Seeing as I'm not a dog owner in New York, that also means everybody else could be something other than what they seem to be. That means it's impossible to know anything at all.

All these people. They are everywhere. On the streets, in the parks, in the shops, in the skyscrapers. What do they do? It's impossible to tell what they do by looking at them.

I suppose they are trying to make it all come together. Just like we do in Norway and everywhere else. They try to make it all work. I see them while they're on their way from one place to the next, torn out of their context. They're on their way elsewhere to make things work there. Things have to work everywhere, and on many levels. It all has to work on a personal level, with the family, at work and with friends, in the local community, and of course globally.

Quite a few things have to gel.

And as I stand there with the dog, at an intersection on the east side of Manhattan, I wonder whether all this will ever gel for me. Will I make it?

I don't think I am any different from other people. I have the same dreams. I want a family. I want a house. A car. Why shouldn't I want that? Everybody does. And when I have it, I want it all to work.

I feel I am starting to care about all these people. I understand them. Of course they have to walk here in the street, they have to get somewhere. Things have to work everywhere. I am thinking, we're in this together. Keep it up. It's going to be just fine.

Hopi

I keep nagging my brother to take us up the Empire State Building. He says we're going to do it on a sunny day with clear weather. We walk and we walk. We look at houses, at people and cars. Shops. We eat and drink. I've bought a bunch of very small bananas. We've walked tens of kilometres, and I've got a new pair of shoes, because the old ones were giving me blisters. It was very sore. I got a pair of Nikes. Hiking boots. My brother paid for them with one of his credit cards.

I always buy Nike. And Levi's. I think they're the best. I really do. I don't even consider buying other brands. Somebody must have done their job very well.

My brother is interested in art. I didn't know that. There are many things I don't know about him. But it's good that we're together. Even though he sometimes gets a little stern. We walk around in SoHo for a while. Visiting galleries. I see plans for a project that has tremendous appeal to me.

Somebody is thinking of building a massive concrete structure over the San Andreas Fault in California. It is a sculpture. It'll be eighty metres long and sixty metres wide. And seven metres tall. It will be built with a type of concrete claimed to be the most durable material there is. The slab will weigh

65,000 tonnes. But the ground on which it's going to stand is moving. Quite fast. The concrete slab will be torn in half, and the two parts will drift apart at a speed of 6–9 cm a year. In 43 million years the left part of the slab will be where Alaska is today. This is art with a purpose. All projects ought to be like this.

In another gallery I find a folder about Einstein. Made by an art student. She has read a lot about Einstein and found information about him and gathered it all in a folder called the Einstein Papers. I want to buy it. It costs 20 dollars. My brother thinks it's foolish, of course. He tries to talk me out of it. But Einstein is my friend. I buy the folder. My brother is shaking his head.

Now my brother stands pointing at the Empire State Building. I can see it. It towers in the landscape. And the top floors are illuminated by a blue light. I want us to go there. Now. But my brother has made other plans. It is late. He thinks we should go home and watch TV.

We drink a beer, while a woman on TV is saying that if I have an accident, I should call her and she will help me make a court case and get money from those responsible for the accident or from those who own the ground on which the accident happened. She makes it sound so simple.

In bed, I read the Einstein Papers. It's just twenty-odd sheets of A4 paper. Some photographs and a bit of writing here and there. Claire, who made the folder, writes that Einstein was a kind man who cared about people, and that he was very concerned that science should be a blessing to humanity. Einstein had two aspirations in life, it says. The first was to lead a simple life. The second was to formulate a theory that could express the interconnectedness of nature, and which would ultimately lead to peace and justice for all.

One of the sheets is a copy of one of the manuscript pages on which Einstein wrote his theory. I look respectfully at the sheet. Some words and some figures. Maybe this is where it says that time doesn't quite exist. The sheet looks like this:

Albert Einstein, 6 1/4 page autograph manuscript of his paper, *Eincheitliche Feldtheorie und Hamilton'sches Prinzip*, 1929.

SWANN GALLERIES

from my study of Einstein   Claire Wankel

The best thing in the folder is a picture of Einstein together with a group of Indians. Einstein is smiling and wearing feathers on his head. And it says that the Hopi Indians are the best suited to understand the theory of relativity. Their language does not have a word for time, and the concepts of past and future do not exist. They don't see time as linear, but as a circular space where past, present and future exist side by side. When I get home, I want to check and see if there is a Hopi community in Oslo, and whether I can frequent it even though I'm not a Hopi.

Before I go to sleep, I write down what I remember the most from my first two days in this city:

- A man in uniform who came running out of a building to carry the luggage for an elegantly dressed woman getting out of a taxi
- Four Asian-looking boys playing volleyball on the grass in a park
- A man playing classical guitar in a subway station
- A large area cordoned off due to a burst water main
- A boy running in a park while his dad was trying to get him interested in a stick
- A shop window full of inflatable cushions
- A big man speaking Russian and frying hamburgers in a huge lump of butter
- A big bottle of beer
- A man on rollerblades who first almost crashed into a lady and who, a minute later, almost crashed into a car
- An orthodox Jew with a walkman and red trainers
- A girl giving away samples of a new brand of chewing gum, who said it was free today only
- A man sitting with a notice which said that he didn't have any money and that he was HIV-positive

- A girl who came into a shop and asked the man behind the counter how he was doing
- A lady in sunglasses sitting in a cafe telling her friend that she'd been talking to a man until four o'clock in the morning and that it was a relationship she had faith in
- A restaurant owner standing in the street swinging a golf club while we were eating dinner
- A very long car that had tinted, black windows so nobody could look inside
- A Chinese porno magazine where the cover girl was holding a hand over her nipples

1-800-PARKS

When I wake up, Obi has pulled all my little bananas off the kitchen counter. They're all over the floor. I shake my head and say Obi, Obi. David still hasn't been here. He should have come two days ago.

Someone will have to walk Obi. I have to walk Obi. I put on my new Nike shoes. Now Obi and I are going out. It's raining.

By the entrance to the park there is a sign with a phone number you can call if you have a Parks-related problem. In a way, Obi is such a problem. I take down the phone number: 1-800-Parks. If David doesn't pick Obi up by the end of the day, I'm going to call it.

A man with a dog calls from afar asking whether Obi is a he or a she. It is obvious that his dog is a she and that it is in heat. It's running loose as well. I shout back saying that I don't know. The man looks at me shaking his head. He thinks I'm weird.

Now I meet another man with a dog. He knows Obi, he says. He says Obi has a high metabolism, and that I should feed Obi more often than he feeds his dog. It is a meaningless piece of information. He doesn't say anything about how often he feeds his dog. But he tells me that Obi is a he.

I have only brought one bag, so when Obi sits down to crap for a second time, he makes me embarrassed. He's crapping on the pavement. When he is done, we cross the street and pretend nothing happened.

Shame on you, I say to Obi. *Bad dog.*

Walking a dog in the streets of New York is absurd. But it gives me perspective. Lots of it. I'm so far away from home. In a big city. All the people. And I am only one. The only thing I can be sure of at any given time is what I am thinking myself. I have no idea what the others are thinking. Do they think space is big and dangerous? I do. What do they believe in? I think nobody ought to be alone. That one should be with someone. With friends. With the person one loves. I think it is important to love. I think it's the most important thing.

While my brother's preparing breakfast, I write a postcard to Lise.

This is what I am writing:

Hi Lise,

New York is so big. I get a bit of the same feeling as I do with space. That I am exempt from responsibility. That there is nothing I can do except to try and have a good time. I am walking a dog named Obi. We live in an apartment with a doorman. He has a uniform and says how are you today, mister, and I say fine. My brother doesn't want me to talk about time or space. I look forward to seeing you. I haven't hammered since I last saw you. I think the most important thing is to love.

When I return from posting the card, Obi is gone. David has been to fetch him. I don't have to call 1-800-Parks.

I ask my brother what David said, but he tells me that David hardly said a thing. He just apologised for being two days late and then he asked if the little bananas were real ones.

In America they don't know if fruit lying on the floor is real or plastic.

While we eat, my brother asks me what I think.

About what? I say.

About all of it, he says.

I tell him about the perspective I just experienced, and that I think New York is a little like space and that the most important thing is to love.

My brother nods. He asks me whether I have ever considered thinking less.

I tell him I consider it all the time, but that it's not that easy.

My brother says I should spend more time doing things that can only be experienced.

Like what, for instance? I say.

Play, he says. And he says that today I must let him decide.

I ask him what he is deciding.

He is deciding that we'll be doing little thinking and lots of laughing.

Fine by me, I say.

The Library

We are sitting in the New York Public Library. My brother decided that we'd go here. It's a great library. Big. Lots of people. And guards making sure those leaving haven't stolen any books. I am looking at periodicals. In an issue of *Time* I see a picture of a gas cloud somewhere in the universe. The picture is taken by a satellite and the caption explains that the gas cloud is several trillion kilometres tall. This is the way it's supposed to be.

My brother is sitting at the other end of the room, facing a computer. I can see he is laughing to himself. He waves me over. Directly opposite my brother a hobo sits reading. All his bags are standing on the floor. Probably fifteen bags. And his clothes are just rags. But he is reading a book called *Economic Science*.

The woman in the elevator in the hotel in Oslo was right when she said the world is more complex than I think. But my brother isn't that complex. He is sitting there searching for authors who have Norwegian taboo words for names. Now he's typing a very bad word. He laughs and laughs. I think it's a bit silly. But when the result comes up, I start laughing, too. It is terribly childish, but quite gratifying. I get sucked into it. And while I laugh, I am looking around hoping nobody realises what we're up to.

We sit there for a long while. Maybe an hour. It is a magnificent experience. I haven't laughed this hard in ages. The fun often lies in the gap between the authors' names and the serious nature of what they've written. But sometimes I find it satisfying just to see the words appear on the screen. I feel we're playing a trick on someone. My brother and I are outdoing each other in coming up with words. Some of them are pretty bad.

Here is some of what we find:

You searched for the AUTHOR: **fitte** = Cunt
10 AUTHORS found with 28 ENTRIES

1. Fitte Albert
2. Fitte Ernesto J (14 entries)
3. Fitter Alastair (2 entries)
4. Fitter Chris
5. Fitter E Ingles Joseph
6. Fitter Jorn Carsten (2 entries)
7. Fitter Richard Sidney Richmond (3 entries)
8. Fitterer Mario
9. Fitterling Thomas
10. Fitterman Robert (2 entries)

(EXTENDED DISPLAY)- (START OVER)- (ANOTHER SEARCH)- (LIMIT/SORT)

The Research Libraries of The New York Public Library/All Locations   http://149.123.101.18/search/wfitte/0,9,9/item&wfitte&6,6,9

Call #   HKR 73-2509
Author   Fitte, Ernesto J.
Title   Martín García; historia de una isla argentina [por] Ernesto J. Fitte.
Imprint   Buenos Aires, Emecé Editores [1971]

Descript   207 p. map. 21 cm.
Note   "Adhesión a las IIas. Jornadas de Historia del Litoral Fluvial Argentino."
            Includes bibliographical references.
Subject   Martín García (Island) --History.

The Research Libraries of The New York Public Library/All Locationhttp://149.123.101.18/search/afitte/0,10,28/item&afitte+albert&1,0,0

(NEXT RECORD)- (PREVIOUS RECORD)- (RETURN TO BROWSE)- (ANOTHER SEARCH)-
(START OVER)
You searched for the AUTHOR: fitte = Cunt

Author Fitte, Albert.
Title   **Spectroscopie d'une propagande révolutionnaire : "El Moudjahid" des temps de guerre;
        juin 1956-mars 1962 / Albert Fitte.**
Imprint Montpellier : Université Paul Valéry, [Centre d'histoire militaire de Montpellier], 1973.

Descriptiv 160, iv, 150 p. ; 25 cm.
Series Études militaires. 1
Note   "Répertoire pour la consultation des trois volumes de la reédition d'el Moudjahid": p. 1-150
        (4th group).
        Includes bibliographical references.
Subject el-Moudjahid.
        Algeria --History --1945-1962.

(NEXT RECORD)- (PREVIOUS RECORD)- (RETURN TO BROWSE)- (ANOTHER SEARCH)-
(START OVER)

You searched for the AUTHOR: **kuk** = cock
163 AUTHORS found with 298 ENTRIES

1. Kuk D Ben Nahum Ha Kohen
2. Kuk G I
3. Kuk Leszek
4. Kuk Shalom Natan Raanan 1900 1972
5. Kuk Yehudit
6. Kukacarna Va
7. Kukacka Helmut
8. Kukacka L E
9. Kukacka Lawrence E
10. Kukacka Miroslav

(NEXT PAGE)- (EXTENDED DISPLAY)- (START OVER)- (ANOTHER SEARCH)- (LIMIT/SORT)

The Research Libraries of The New York Public Library/All Locathttp://149.123.101.18/search/akuk/0,163,298/item&akuk+yehudit&1,5,0

(NEXT RECORD)- (PREVIOUS RECORD)- (RETURN TO BROWSE)- (ANOTHER SEARCH)-
(START OVER)
You searched for the AUTHOR: kuk = cock

Call # *PBP 82-2639
Author Kuk, Yehudit.
Title MH'SBT YHWDYT : KTBY/M / YHWDYT QWQ ; [HTQYN WHBYA LDPWS
'SMWAL MRW/M].
Imprint YRW'SLY/M : [s.n.], 738 [1978]

Descript 197 p. ; 25 cm.
Subject Bible. O.T. Genesis --Meditations.
Judaism.
Add'l name Marom, Shemuel.
Donor Mahashevet Yehudit.

(NEXT RECORD)- (PREVIOUS RECORD)- (RETURN TO BROWSE)- (ANOTHER SEARCH)-
(START OVER)

The Research Libraries of The New York Public Library/All Locations

You searched for the AUTHOR: pikk = *dick*
3 AUTHORS found with 3 ENTRIES

1. Pikkert P
2. Pikkusaari Jussi 1939
3. Pikkuvirta V G

(EXTENDED DISPLAY)- (START OVER)- (ANOTHER SEARCH)- (LIMIT/SORT)

You searched for the KEYWORDS: **suging** = Sucking
Found 2 items:
SUGII is in 2 titles.
There are 2 entries with SUGII.

☐ Kindai Nihon shakai to Kirisutokyo / Sugii Mutsuro Sensei Ta(1989)
☐ Kindai Nihon shakai to Kirisutokyo / Sugii Mutsuro Sensei Ta(1989)

(EXTENDED DISPLAY)- (RETURN TO BROWSE)- (START OVER)- (ANOTHER SEARCH)-
(LIMIT/SORT)

The Research Libraries of The New York Public Library/All I.http://149.123.101.18/search/asug...bot+of+saint+denis+1081+1151&1,,3

(NEXT RECORD)- (RETURN TO BROWSE)- (ANOTHER SEARCH)- (START OVER)

Call # MQN 80-1764
        JFD 80-10174 --Additional copy.
Author Suger, Abbot of Saint Denis, 1081-1151.
Title   **Abbot Suger on the Abbey Church of St.-Denis and its art treasures / edited, translated,
        and annotated by Erwin Panofsky. 2d ed. / by Gerda Panofsky-Soergel.**
Imprint Princeton, N.J. : Princeton University Press, c1979

Descript xix, 285 [28] p. : ill. ; 25 cm.
Note   Latin and English.
          Bibliography: p. 262-275.
          Includes index.

Subject   Architecture --Early works to 1800.
          Art --Early works to 1800.
          Saint-Denis, France (Benedictine abbey).

Add'l name Panofsky, Erwin, 1892-1968.
            Panofsky-Soergel, Gerda, 1929-

(NEXT RECORD)- (RETURN TO BROWSE)- (ANOTHER SEARCH)- (START OVER)

You searched for the AUTHOR: **basj** = crap

No matches found; nearby items are:

- ☐ Basiron Philippe 15th Cent
- ☐ Basisgruppe Vwl Koln
- ☐ Basisgruppe Wik
- ☐ Basista Jakub
- ☐ Basit Abdul 1942-
- ☐ Basiuk V M
- ☐ Basiuk Victor 1932-
- **Your author *Basj* would be here**
- ☐ Bask Katia
- ☐ Baskakov A N Aleksandr Nikolaevich (5 entries)
- ☐ Baskakov Albert Pavlovich
- ☐ Baskakov Aleksandr Nikolaevich
- ☐ Baskakov Eduard Gennadevich

(NEXT PAGE)- (PREVIOUS PAGE)- (EXTENDED DISPLAY)- (START OVER)-
(ANOTHER SEARCH)

Call # *KF(T) 1862 91-249
Author Church of England
Title   Book of common prayer. Hawaiian
          **Ka Buke o ka pule ana a me ka hooko ana i na kauoha hemolele : e like me ka mea i
          kauohaia no ka haipule ana ma ka pae aina Hawaii : ua huiia hoi me na Halelu a Davida, i
          hookaawaleia i mea e himeni ai a heluhelu ai paha ilolo o na halepule.**
Imprint [Honolulu? : s.n.] (Honolulu : Polynesian Book and Job Print.), 1862.

Descript 397 p. ; 19 cm.
Local note Inscribed: "The Hawaiian Prayer Book as translated by the late King of Hawaii Kamehameha
          IV. for Lady Franklin with the love of Emma R."
Note   "He olelo hoakaka" (p. 391-397) dated Honolulu, June, 1863.

You searched for the AUTHOR: **rumpehull**   = bumhole
No matches found; nearby items are:

Rump Erling
Rump Gerhard Charles (3 entries)
Rump Hans Hermann (2 entries)
Rump Hans Uwe 1945
Rump Kabita
Rump Kay 1937
Rump Reinhold 1938
Your author *Rumpehull* would be here
Rumpel Franz
Rumpel Heinrich 1912
Rumpel Johannes
Rumpel Roland
Rumpeters A (2 entries)

(NEXT PAGE)- (PREVIOUS PAGE)- (EXTENDED DISPLAY)- (START OVER)-
(ANOTHER SEARCH)

You searched for the AUTHOR: **runke** = wank
11 AUTHORS found with 19 ENTRIES

1. Runke James F (6 entries)
2. Runkel David R
3. Runkel Gunter 1946
4. Runkel Gunther
5. Runkel Hue Williams Ltd (3 entries)
6. Runkel Kenneth E 1881
7. Runkel Margaret 1906
8. Runkel Otto
9. Runkel Philip Julian 1917
10. Runkel Phillip M
11. Runkel Reinhild (2 entries)

(EXTENDED DISPLAY)- (START OVER)- (ANOTHER SEARCH)- (LIMIT/SORT)

The Research Libraries of The New York Public Library/All Lochttp://149.123.101.18/search/arunke/0,11,19/item&arunke+james+f&3,,6

(NEXT RECORD)- (PREVIOUS RECORD)- (RETURN TO BROWSE)- (ANOTHER SEARCH)- (START OVER)

You searched for the AUTHOR: runke = *wank*

Record 3 of 6

Call # JLF 79-60

Title **Proceedings of the regional rail planning seminars, fall 1976 / edited by James F. Runke and Norbert Y. Zucker.**

Imprint [Washington] : U. S. Dept. of Transportation, Federal Railroad Administration, 1977.

Descript v, 161 p. : ill. ; 29 cm.

Note Cover title: Regional rail planning seminars.

Papers presented at five seminars held in Atlanta, Omaha, Salt Lake City, Fort Worth, and Albany in the fall of 1976 and sponsored by the Federal Railroad Administration, U. S. Dept. of Transportation and the Council of State Governments.

Includes bibliographical references.

Subject Railroads and state --United States --Congresses.

Transportation planning --United States --Congresses.

Add'l name Zucker, Norbert Y.

Runke, James F.

United States. Federal Railroad Administration.

Council of State Governments.

Alt title Regional rail planning seminars.

(NEXT RECORD)- (PREVIOUS RECORD)- (RETURN TO BROWSE)- (ANOTHER SEARCH)- (START OVER)

The Research Libraries of The New York Public Library/All Lochttp://149.123.101.18/search/apupp/apupp/0,23,77/item&apupp+wolfgang&1,1,0

You searched for the AUTHOR: pupp = *tit*

Call #   JSC 73-199
Author Pupp, Wolfgang.
Title   **Vakuumtechnik; Grundlagen und Anwendungen. Vacuum techniques; principles and
         applications. 2. Aufl., neu bearb. und erg.**
Imprint München, K. Thiemig [c1972]

Descript xi, 402 p. illus. 18 cm.
Series   Thiemig-Taschenbücher. Bd. 43
Note   Bibliography: p. 385-393.
Subject   Vacuum technology.
Alt title Vacuum techniques.

You searched for the AUTHOR: **slikke** = Lick
3 AUTHORS found with 5 ENTRIES

1. Slikke Maria Van Der
2. Slikkerveer L J Leendert Jan (3 entries)
3. Slikkerveer Leendert Jan

(EXTENDED DISPLAY)- (START OVER)- (ANOTHER SEARCH)- (LIMIT/SORT)

The Research Libraries of The New York Public Library/All Locati http://149.123.101.18/search/afis/0,1966,4278/item&afis+teodor&1,0,0

(NEXT RECORD)- (PREVIOUS RECORD)- (RETURN TO BROWSE)- (ANOTHER SEARCH)-
(START OVER)
You searched for the AUTHOR: **fis** = *fart*

Call #	*QVM 92-692
Author	Fis, Teodor.
Title	**Dukelské noci.**
Edition	[1. vyd.]
Imprint	Bratislava, Vydavateľstvo politickej literatúry, 1965.
Descript	151 p. front. 21 cm.
Subject	World War, 1939-1945 --Fiction.

(NEXT RECORD)- (PREVIOUS RECORD)- (RETURN TO BROWSE)- (ANOTHER SEARCH)-
(START OVER)

The Research Libraries of The New York Public Library/All Locatiohttp://149.123.101.18/search/arompe/arompe/0,4,5/exact&arompe+robert&1,2

You searched for the AUTHOR: rompe = $arse$
Found 2 items:
Rompe Robert

1. Ergebnisse der Plasmaphysik und der Gaselektronik. (1967)
2. Festschrift des wissenschaftlichen Kolloquiums zum 65. Geburtstag von Robert Rom (1973)

(EXTENDED DISPLAY)- (RETURN TO BROWSE)- (START OVER)- (ANOTHER SEARCH)-
(LIMIT/SORT)

After a while my brother gets up to go and buy some chocolate. I tell him I'll be there in a minute. I tell him there are a few words I want to check. Maybe I've got a guilty conscience since we've just been having fun at other people's expense for so long.

I do a search with some words that are more agreeable. It's not quite as fun, but I feel I am creating a sort of balance.

This is what I find:

You searched for the AUTHOR: **klokke** = Watch
3 AUTHORS found with 5 ENTRIES

1. Klokke A H
2. Klokke Coster A
3. Klokke Marijke J (3 entries)

(EXTENDED DISPLAY)- (START OVER)- (ANOTHER SEARCH)- (LIMIT/SORT)

(NEXT RECORD)- (PREVIOUS RECORD)- (RETURN TO BROWSE)- (ANOTHER SEARCH)-
(START OVER)
You searched for the AUTHOR: klokke = *watch*

Call #   JFL 73-170 [Nr.] 79
Title   **De slimme en de domme : Ngadju-Dajakse volksverhalen / A. Klokke-Coster, A. H.**
          Klokke, M. Saha.
Imprint's-Gravenhage : Nijhoff, 1976.

Descript viii, 121 p. : ill. ; 24 cm.
Series   Instituut voor Taal-, Land- en Volkenkunde. Verhandelingen. \[Nr.] 79\79\
Note   Dutch and Ngadju dialect.
          Bibliography: p. [1].
Subject   Tales. Ngadju --Indonesia --Kalimantan.
Add'l name Klokke-Coster, A.
          Klokke, A. H.
          Saha, Munte.

(NEXT RECORD)- (PREVIOUS RECORD)- (RETURN TO BROWSE)- (ANOTHER SEARCH)-
(START OVER)

You searched for the AUTHOR: **bankebrett** = hammer-and-peg
No matches found; nearby items are:

- Banka Lawrence
- Banka Slovenije (2 entries)
- Bankai Workshop 1992 Brussels Belgium
- Bankaliuk L V
- Bankara Felix
- Bankav A la
- Bankcard Holders Of America

  Your author *Bankebrett* would be here

- Bankei 1622-1693 (2 entries)
- Bankel Hansgeorg (2 entries)
- Bankel Walter
- Bankel Robert
- Bankendorf Carla

-(NEXT PAGE)- -(PREVIOUS PAGE)- -(EXTENDED DISPLAY)- -(START OVER)-
-(ANOTHER SEARCH)

You searched for the AUTHOR: **ball**   = ball
1029 AUTHORS found with 2235 ENTRIES

1. Ball A Gordon
2. Ball Abraham 1908- (3 entries)
3. Ball Adrian (4 entries)
4. Ball Alan
5. Ball Alan M
6. Ball Alan R (6 entries)
7. Ball Alan William (4 entries)
8. Ball Alice Morton
9. Ball Allan Perley 1871-
10. Ball Ann
11. Ball Anthony Michael
12. Ball Arthur E

(NEXT PAGE)- (EXTENDED DISPLAY)- (START OVER)- (ANOTHER SEARCH)- (LIMIT/SORT)

You searched for the AUTHOR: min jente = *my girl*
No matches found; nearby items are:

Min Fan Lu
Min Habar Sh Shelomoh (2 entries)
Min Hsiao Hui Shang Kuan
Min Hyon Gu (2 entries)
Min Il Gi
Min J K
Min J L 1949
     Your author *Min Jente* would be here ----- Change search to Jente, Min
Min Kantrowitz Associates
Min Kwan Sik 1918
Min Kyong Bae (3 entries)
Min Kyong Bae 1934 (2 entries)
Min Kyong Hyon 1933

(NEXT PAGE)- (PREVIOUS PAGE)- (EXTENDED DISPLAY)- (START OVER)-
(ANOTHER SEARCH)

You searched for the AUTHOR: **jente, min**   = *girl, mine*
No matches found; nearby items are:

- Jenssen Pharmaceutica
- Jensson Liv 1906
- Jenstad Margaret A
- Jenster Per V
- Jensterle Alenka
- Jent Louis 1936
- Jent Louis 1936-
- **Your author *Jente Min* would be here** ----- Change search to **Min, Jente,**
- Jentel Marie Odile
- Jentgen Leon
- Jentgen Pierre 1884 (2 entries)
- Jentgens Stephanie
- Jentleson Bruce W 1951 (3 entries)

(NEXT PAGE)- (PREVIOUS PAGE)- (EXTENDED DISPLAY)- (START OVER)-
(ANOTHER SEARCH)

We walk on in the big city. The morning has been a great success. While we were sitting in the library, I hardly had a single thought. I just laughed. I tell my brother he is good at deciding.

Now we're standing in front of the Empire State Building. It's still raining, so we walk past without going up in the elevator. I look at the building. It is enormous. I can't see the top. But I know time passes a little faster up there. I tell my brother, but he thinks it's rubbish.

The Park

This city makes it easy to think about big things. I am thinking about Paul's book. It confuses me. The only question that really counts, must be this one: are things getting better or are they getting worse? That goes for me, and it goes for all human beings, animals, and for the whole world. And all this stuff about what's going to happen in a billion billion years really just doesn't concern me. I suddenly realise. It might be egotistical, but I am more concerned about what's going to happen while I am alive than about what's going to happen afterwards. Thinking about this is an enormous liberation. The thought comes to me while my brother and I are throwing frisbee in Central Park. We've been throwing for a long while. We keep moving further and further apart. My brother has bought a very good frisbee. It's heavy and stable. Sometimes I feel I could throw it as far as infinity. Now I'm throwing. Now my brother's catching. Now my brother's throwing. Now I'm catching.

It's been several minutes since either of us dropped the frisbee on the ground. My brother is very involved. He runs as fast as he can. He's jumping and throwing himself all over the place. His eagerness is affecting me. I am thinking I will never stop throwing things. I am thinking that I believe in cleansing the soul through fun and games.

Dumber

It is evening and my body is tired from all the playing and walking. I am really pooped.

Like I used to be when we got home from skiing trips when I was little. And I've got a blister from the frisbee. It's on the outside of the right index finger. In a while I will pop a hole in the blister, clean it and put a Donald Duck plaster on it. There are lots of Donald Duck plasters in the bathroom cupboard.

My brother asks me if I am happy with my day and I say yes. I tell him I want to play more tomorrow. He smiles at me and says there's a good boy. He says I must wean myself from all the scary thoughts. Forget all that stuff about space, he says.

Now he is serving me Japanese take-away and turning on the TV. Today it's about a boy who used to be skinny when he was in high school. The girls didn't think he was particularly cool and when he asked the prettiest girl in class to a party, she said no.

Now a few years have passed, and the boy has become totally different. He has a moustache and muscles. He is running around on stage showing off his big biceps. The audience is cheering. And he has a girlfriend who is prettier than the prettiest girl in class used to be. And the girl who was the prettiest girl in class is also coming on stage. Now she's sorry. The show is about the fact that looks don't count as much as what we're like inside.

I think Americans are a little dumber than I am. My brother thinks so, too. I'm sure Dad does as well.

This is what I have seen today:

– A black man calling his bike *bitch*
– A shop where they sold fire-fighter equipment
– A painting by Dali where some clocks were hanging as though they had melted
– Two men wearing yarmulkas running out of an ambulance
– Five black youths walking in the park, each with a tape recorder on his shoulder. They were talking to each other, but none of them could have heard anything but the music
– A skyscraper that hadn't been finished
– A little boy smoking drugs in a park
– A shop that had so many periodicals I had to give up
– An older, unshaven man and a rather young woman who sat leaning against each other on a bench, sleeping
– A bike shop with my favourite bike
– A skinny old man with his tie over his shoulder shouting loudly at a car jumping a red light
– A woman assistant in a jeans shop who didn't have anything to do
– A policeman on a bike, with a gun
– A black man drumming on empty paint tins, a bread bin and an oven griddle. He was incredibly good and I gave him money
– A man who drank coffee while walking down the street

- A man giving an address in Paris to a girl he didn't know
- A fitness centre where people were jogging on treadmills while watching four TV screens
- A bouquet of roses lying all over the street
- A garbage bin full of chopped-off pig's and cow's feet
- A little girl throwing a ball against a wall, while her dad stood behind her saying she was good
- A woman who got cross when she discovered she had made me a vanilla ice cream, when what I had asked for was a chocolate ice cream

Close

I feel I am on a high. For the first time in a very long while I have a feeling that anything can happen. This morning I woke up thinking everything could happen, that things would just come to me, and that they would be good. I haven't felt this way since I was little. It could be this city that's doing it. It could also be my brother. For a while I thought he wasn't quite as friendly as I am. Now I don't think so any more.

He is a good guy. He wishes me well. We've spent a lot of quality time together these last few days.

We've been throwing frisbee and running on the grass. We've talked about what things were like when we were little, and arrived at the fact that they were different. Things were simple, big, but above all different. And sometimes things were better than they are now, and other times they were worse. My brother thinks claiming that everything used to be better is a dead-end street. But different is a word he enjoys. And last night I got him to hammer.

We switched the TV off and sat talking. About girls. My brother has been a bit vague about girls for a while now. He both wants and doesn't want them. I tell him he can't do that. He can't both have a girl and not have her. Not at the same time. At least not unless she is willing to both have and not have him.

He told me about the last girl he went out with. It looked as though they were going to go all the way. But then my brother changed his mind and ruined it all. And the worst thing is that he never quite understood why he did it. It was just a feeling. He thought things might be better with another girl. It was OK as it was, but it might be even better. With someone else. Then he walked out. And now he regrets it. Every day.

After he had said that, he became all quiet and sat there for a long time just shaking his head. I felt sorry for him. I fetched the hammer-and-peg and placed it carefully on the table in front of him. Then I gave him the hammer, and when he took it and gave me a puzzled look, I nodded slowly. Then he started hammering. In a quiet and uncomplicated rhythm he knocked all the pegs down and turned the board over several times. Neither of us said anything. I felt we were really close while he was hammering.

The Owl and the Pussycat

Today we are walking by ourselves a little. My brother on his side and I on mine. We're going to meet later on, but both of us felt that it could be good to be alone for a while.

I am sitting on a bench looking at all the people. It's good for me to see so many other people who are not me. That there are so many others. I feel affection for them. Most of them are doing the best they can. I am also doing the best I can.

I see quite a few who aren't so well off. People who are poor or sad. We ought to be nicer to each other. Not just in America. People all over the world ought to be nicer to each other. Now I am getting up to start talking to people who walk by. Many of them ignore me, but some talk back. I ask them what means something to them.

Some say love.

Some say friends.

Some say my family.

One says music.

One says cars.

One says money, but I can tell he's a sarcastic twit.

One says girls.

Two say *boys*.

Several say both *friends and family*.

Some say they don't know.

I also ask whether they think it will all be all right in the end. Several of them just shake their head at my question, but of those who reply, half of them say *yes* and the other half *no*. I wonder whether this is representative of the remaining population.

I buy a milk shake and slurp down the contents while I walk. My new shoes are super. Nikes are super. This city is full of product names. Partly because there are so many billboards, but also because many companies have offices here.

Now I am walking past the Rolex building. I ask the doorman if it is possible to go inside and look at watches, but he says the only thing they've got in there is a workshop. It must be an enormous workshop. But he treats me politely. Maybe I look like I could afford a Rolex.

Now that I have become aware of them, I see billboards everywhere. It's very strange, but I am emotionally attached to the following companies and products, and some of them I have come to love outright:

   — Nike

   — Levi's

   — Volvo

   — Snapple

   — Ray Ban

   — Brio

   — Nikon

   — Sony

   — Findus

   — Cannondale

   — Rolex

- REMA 1000
- Carhart
- Colgate
- BBC
- Berghaus
- Universal Pictures
- NRK
- Urtekram
- Farris
- Statoil
- Apple Macintosh
- SAS
- Sørlandschips
- Absolut Vodka
- Atomic
- Fjällräven
- Solo
- Bang & Olufsen
- Europcar
- Stüssy
- Massey Ferguson

It's not just about advertising. Several of these companies make products I've never seen advertised. I associate them with something good without having any idea why. Some sympathies I have inherited, naturally. REMA 1000 for example. Dad loves REMA 1000. He buys everything there. Even his sleeping bag. But Statoil and Massey Ferguson? I have no idea where I got them from. Either their marketing is so clever that it creates a false idea that I am coming up with it myself, or my personality is more open to certain product names than it is to others. Maybe it has to do with the fact that it is easier to choose once and for all than to be confused every time you buy something new. I'll probably never buy a tractor, but if I do, it's going to be a Massey Ferguson. That's just the way it is.

I am writing a card to Lise asking her what kind of tractor she'd buy.

As I sit on a bench finishing off my milk shake, I have an idea. It is a business idea. These capitalist surroundings are inspiring me. My idea is a telephone service. I want to look into the possibilities for creating one. But I want it to be nice. Most of these telephone services are gross and unpleasant. They appeal to the dark side in us, to people like Kent, my bad friend. They appeal to our urges and our fear of loneliness. I want to create a telephone service with a difference. A pleasant one. A help-line for people who just need a little break. For people who, for a few minutes, need to feel that the world is good. I'm going to ask Børre to sing The Owl and the Pussycat on tape. It's a good song.

> The owl and the Pussy-cat went to sea,
> In a beautiful pea-green boat . . .
> The owl looked up to the stars above,
> And sang to a small guitar,
> "Oh lovely Pussy, Pussy my love,
> What a beautiful Pussy you are"

I am going to open a premium-rate 829-number, pay Børre a one-off fee, maybe a thousand kroner, and then I'll advertise in a national newspaper and charge those who call twelve or fifteen kroner a minute. It could make me some money. And I feel certain that such a service will fill a gap. That there's a market for it.

We all have our melancholy moments. Days when the feeling of meaninglessness creeps in and we sink into cynicism and sarcasm. Days when we stop believing in love and that everything will be all right in the end. At moments like those it would be a blessing to hear the frail and unsteady voice of a child singing a sweet song. If such a telephone service had existed already, I would have been an active user myself. Maybe I would have already made it through this tough spot.

A warm, friendly telephone service. I am creating a niche. And if it works, I'll expand with more songs. Goosy Goosy Gander, Old McDonald Had a Farm, Hickory Dickory Dock. The list is long.

I want to mention this to my brother. Maybe he can throw in some start-up funds, and if it takes off, I'll pay him back generously. The idea is not to get rich. I don't need much for subsistence. I just want to be OK, and then I'd like to have a decent watch.

If the surplus were to become significant, I could donate money to a charitable organisation. I am very happy with this idea. It's strange that I had to go all the way to America to think of it.

The Helmet

I have taken a bicycle helmet. It is a nice helmet. Blue. The
first thirty minutes I was very pleased that I had finally
acquired a helmet. And I was looking forward to showing it
to Børre. But right now it's not so pleasant any more. The
whole thing is a bit bad. The helmet isn't mine. I have taken
something that doesn't belong to me. My brother quickly
made it very clear that he didn't want anything to do with
the helmet, but that he wouldn't interfere with my choices.
I am thinking about my grandfather and his story about the
apple tree and the boys.

I feel like a shady person. Weak, even.

Taking the helmet came so naturally. I think that's what
scares me. My brother and I were coming out of a big museum
where we had been looking at stuffed animals and objects
from all over the world.

I was excited, talking about dinosaurs and whales and
African mammals. I was also talking about a big, black man
who had asked me to take a picture of him in front of the big
brown bear from Alaska. He knew everything about bears and
had great respect for them. He had told me that if I had to
crash-land a plane in Alaska, I'd have to stay far away from the

brown bears. You see, they can run at 35 miles an hour, and kill a man with a single blow.

While I was describing this to my brother, we went past a parked car with a bicycle helmet sitting on the bumper. I stopped dead. Then I looked around, and a moment later I had constructed a story to justify how the helmet was now mine.

I figured it was obvious that a cyclist had dropped his helmet in the street and that someone had picked it up and left it on the car, so that it wouldn't get run over by a bus or some other vehicle. I also thought I had saved the helmet by taking it, whereas if I'd left it there, it would definitely have fallen off and got crushed when the car drove off. Then I took the helmet and put it in my bag, and continued chatting to my brother about entirely different things. But as time passed, I felt the helmet getting heavier and heavier, and by the time we got home it was really heavy.

Just now I discovered a name and a phone number on the inside of the helmet. That doesn't make things easier. The owner suddenly has a name. His name is José, and I imagine that he has fled from Cuba and has just got his green card. But he probably doesn't have a job. He's only just getting by. And the helmet has definitely been given to him as a present. Having to deal with this is really unpleasant.

Most of all I feel like sinking deep into a thick book about chaos theory, but the helmet is lying here on my bedside table insisting on its presence. I've even had it on my head.

The whole situation is a bit pathetic. I have to return the helmet, but it's too late to phone José tonight. Now I am putting the helmet on the floor, so that I won't have to see it the moment I wake up.

This is what I have seen today:

– A man in a white shirt lighting a cigarette on a stone

staircase while relaxing for the first time in a long while (at least that's what it looked like)

- A telephone booth where two receivers were dangling from their cords
- A man with a Walkman who hurried through the part of the natural history museum which dealt with the evolution of the human race
- A boy in a cafe who kept looking out into space every time his girlfriend said something, but who wanted her to look at him whenever he said something
- A man combing his beard
- A man who was playing a harmonica in the middle of the street and who hardly twitched when he almost got run over by a truck
- A family of three fat Germans asking if there was an elevator up to the first floor of a McDonald's restaurant
- A man holding hands with another man
- A police woman who stood for a long time gazing at an apple
- A woman who said *please leave me alone* when I asked if she needed help to carry her bags up a flight of stairs

The Note

I can't sleep. I am thinking about how keeping the helmet is incompatible with being a really good guy. And when I finally fall asleep, I dream that nobody likes me. It's a bad night. The first thing I do when I wake up is to call José. I tell him who I am and that I've found the helmet and that he can pick it up from the doorman at the address where I live. José is very glad. He thinks it's generous of me to call. He never thought he'd get the helmet back. People in New York are like wolves, he says. I say it's only right and that he must think no more of it.

My brother is proud of me, and wants to buy me breakfast at a Chinese restaurant nearby. I'm grinning from ear to ear. Suddenly I'm having the best time. I imagine that I am feeling better now that I have returned the helmet, than I would have had I never taken it. It's really weird that way.

I eat noodles and talk about my plans for the Owl and the Pussycat phone line. My brother is a bit sceptical, but not dismissive, and he doesn't exclude the possibility of contributing with some start-up capital.

When we've finished our food, a young Chinese girl comes over with a tray that she sets down on the table. On the tray lie the bill and two small cookies. Inside the cookies we find a piece of paper each with a little prediction on it.

On my brother's note it says: *You are the center of every group's attention.*

My note says: *You will be advanced socially without any special effort.*

It's a fantastic thought. In many ways a cushion. It does not inspire me to action in any way. But it's good. I won't have to do anything at all. And I'll still get something back. It doesn't get any better than that.

Many

One can say a lot of things about New York, but I feel convinced that it is one of the few places in the world where you can have fun even when you don't try.

Today a lot of things have happened. Four of them have to do with time.

First I found this postcard.

Then I saw an advertisement in the *New York Times*. It was Tiffany & Co. advertising a watch called the Tiffany Tesoro watch. It costs 7500 dollars. If enough people call the Owl and the Pussycat phone line, I might be able to buy it. I think the ad text is really good. Especially the bit about the sound of gold. My brother liked it too.

> *What we remember*
> *is what touches our heart.*
> *A certain gesture.*
> *The play of light.*
> *The sound of gold.*
> *The very moment itself.*

A little later, when my brother and I were on our way to a museum, we passed a girl writing poetry for money. She said that if I'd give her anything between five dollars and twenty dollars, she would write me a poem. I gave her seven dollars and said it had to be about time. She spent ten minutes writing. She wrote a nice little poem. I can see how one could probably have done some more work on it, but one shouldn't always be so critical and opinionated. And the girl seemed very friendly.

Here's the poem:

Time

Held here in the
hour glass of your
arms, sand cascading
through the body
of our love
I am,
temporarily suspended
out of time
in the comfort of
your skin,
the surety of
Knowing when I turn over,
my elbow will jostle
your elbow.
And the sand
running through the
hourglass
is

from the
Beach of Eternity
And will never
Run Dry.

The fourth thing that had to do with time, I experienced at the Museum of Television and Radio. My brother was sitting watching some old TV programme. He was taking far too long, and I was getting bored.

I sat down in front of a computer and started pressing keys at random. I don't know what I wrote, but it might have been *Time* or perhaps *Timex*. Whatever it was, a selection of watch advert descriptions came up. It hit the spot. I do want a watch. I sat there for a while reading synopses of watch commercials. It was good. Now I feel that I'll be more capable of choosing a watch, when that day comes.

Here are a few of the synopses.

The first one:
This commercial shows how Citizen is a wristwatch with style, and that it appeals to sophisticated men and women. Photographs are shown of men and women preparing to meet each other while the song 'About a Quarter to Nine' is played on the soundtrack.
Slogan: *No other watch expresses time as beautifully*.

The second one:
In this commercial for Seiko, several men and women explain that their Seiko watches have given them completely reliable time indications for years. They all agree that their Seiko watches have been worth every krone.
Slogan: *Man invented time. Seiko perfected it*.

The third one:
In this commercial for Swatch, a young woman is listening to a taped Italian lesson, while sitting in her bedroom putting on nail polish.

The fourth one:
In this commercial for Timex, we see a giant wristwatch together with pictures of people at work and at play. A voice-over explains that Timex have created a collection of watches the user can be proud of. Whether you need a watch for sporting activities, leisure or the business world, Timex will have something to suit your needs.
Slogan: *Bring the value of Timex Quartz into your world.*

The fifth one:
In this commercial for Timex, John Cameron Swayze goes to Acapulco to test how waterproof a Timex really is. While Swayze is watching, the world champion diver, Paul Garcia, jumps off the top of the most famous cliff in Acapulco, La Perla, with a Timex on his wrist. When he surfaces again, the watch is still working. Is it surprising that more people buy Timex than any other watch in the world, Swayze asks?
Slogan: *It took a licking and kept on ticking.*

The sixth one:
In this black/white commercial for TAG Heuer Sports Watches, swimmers and athletes are shown battling against the clock.
Slogan: *Success is a mind game.*

The seventh one:
In this commercial for Seiko we are shown a series of pictures of men and women with a lot of responsibility both at home and at work.
Slogan: *When people are counting on you, you can count on Seiko.*

I was a bit disappointed that Rolex wasn't featured, and that it didn't say anything about atomic clocks. But Timex, Seiko and TAG-Heuer appealed to me. It's about not going for just any watch. I wonder what type of watch Paul has got. He probably has a good one. Maybe he's got an atomic clock. As far as ordinary citizens are likely to have atomic clocks, Paul is probably one of them.

Lucky pig.

I don't often experience four things that all have to do with time. At least not all in one day. It will probably be a while before it happens again. And I've also seen a lot of other things. I am starting to become saturated.

This is what I have seen:
- An elderly man who thanked me and called me brother for giving him money for the subway fare
- A Vietnamese waiter who tried to explain to my brother that the one crab on the menu was hard and the other one was soft
- A street not far from Wall Street that was closed off while a lot of stock brokers were playing baseball
- A Latin American cycling in far too low a gear
- A TV report about the guitar brand Fender, where a heavy rocker said that a Fender is like a woman, that it must be treated gently and with respect
- A group of men in their 40s playing basketball, none of whom was as good as Dad
- Clint Eastwood arriving at the Museum of Modern Art in a limousine
- A man in an expensive suit who laughed, looking at some coins he was carrying in his hand
- A well-dressed woman saying asshole to a cyclist
- An elderly black man sitting guard in front of an elevator,

who was shouting something to another man, a friend
passing by, wearing a green uniform
- A woman who asked; *are you going to make someone happy?*
when I bought flowers for the people whose apartment
we are borrowing
- A girl on TV who was crying because her mum had never
been good to her, but who had said instead that she was
fat and ugly and that she didn't want to see her any more
- A man yawning a big yawn
- An exhibition where an artist had painted very many
pictures of a blue dog
- A black man in a red outfit on Times Square shouting
in a microphone: *Where is the love in our society today? There is
no love*

The Building

Now my brother and I are playing Kim's game. It's the one
where you first display some objects lying on the floor or on
a table, and then you cover them with a piece of cloth, and
then the other one has to remember what they were.

We've agreed that the winner gets to decide what we are
going to do today. I remembered everything, but my brother
forgot quite a few things.

This is what he didn't remember:
– His own keyring bunny
– A beer-bottle top
– A subway token
– A balloon

It is always unpleasant to forget obvious things. When I
removed the piece of cloth after he had given up, and he saw
the keyring bunny, he just said oh! the keyring bunny! in a
way that made me understand that he was pretty disappointed
with his effort. I consoled him by saying that he's so much
better at all kinds of other things. Everybody is good at something. My brother sulked for a while, but we've put it behind
us now.

We are on our way to the Empire State Building. As we

approach it, I try to tell my brother how time and gravity are connected, but every time I open my mouth, he raises his right hand and shakes his head to shut me up. While my brother is buying the tickets, I take down the number for a coin-operated telephone on the ground floor: 502 5803. I have a plan. I'm not going to mention it to my brother.

We have to queue to get to the elevator. An elderly lady standing in front of me has a brochure with facts about the building. I peer over her shoulder. It says it's 443 metres tall and that it has 77 elevators that travel at between 200 and 400 metres per minute. I know very well that the Empire State Building is not the tallest in the world. It's not even the tallest in New York City.

A few days ago there was an article on skyscrapers in the *New York Times*. It said the Petronas Towers in Malaysia is the tallest building in the world right now. It is the first time in over a hundred years that America hasn't held the record. Sears Tower in Chicago has for a long time been the tallest, but a body called the Council on Tall Buildings and Urban Habitat has just decided that TV aerials are no longer going to count when measuring height, and that makes the building in Malaysia the tallest. Soon the World Financial Center in Shanghai will be finished, and then that'll be the tallest.

The leader for the Council on Tall Buildings and Urban Habitat, Dr Lynn Beedle, refused to call this a sad moment for American architecture, the article said. And he was quoted having said; *No, no, no, there are still many great things about American buildings. Oh, many, many, great things.*

To me none of this really matters. The Empire State Building is the biggest. It's the one I've seen in movies. It's the one in the middle of New York City. It's the one Paul writes about. The other ones can be as tall as they like.

Now we're taking the elevator. After a few seconds I feel my ears go thick. The digital counter inside the elevator only counts every tenth floor. It goes from fifty to sixty in just a few seconds. Paul should see me now. I feel like clapping my hands.

The view is fantastic. I can see everything. The sea. The city. The mountains on the horizon.

My brother is very systematic. He is taking his time, and he is reading in the guide book about what lies in the various directions. He wants to point and explain, but I move away a little.

I find a phone and make sure my brother can't see me. I'm dialling the number to the payphone on the ground floor now. It's ringing. When someone answers, I plan to ask whether he or she is aware that time passes a little faster up here with me than down there with them.

It rings and rings. For a long time. Nobody is answering. It's bloody annoying. I let it ring just a little longer. Now there's a man picking up the receiver.

Hello? he says.

Hello, I'm calling from the top of the building, I say.

Yes? says the man.

Are you aware that time runs slightly faster at the top than it does at the bottom of this building? I ask.

No, says the man.

Well, it does, I tell him.

All right, says the man.

Are you impressed? I ask.

Not really, he says.

But that means that time doesn't exist, I tell him.

Oh yeah? says the man.

So what do you think? I ask.

I couldn't care less, says the man, and hangs up the receiver. Idiot.

For revenge I drop a coin into one of the binoculars and focus on the street below. It's full of people and cars. I see a man coming out of a bank. He is trying to hail a taxi while at the same time glancing at his watch.

He looks like you and me. Completely ordinary. He probably has a wife and kids and a little house in the suburbs. He is doing everything the best he can. I follow him with my gaze, thinking; I can see you, but you can't see me. We shall never meet, but there is something I want you to know. My time is not the same as your time. Our times are not the same. And do you know what that means? That means that time does not exist. Do you want me to repeat that? There is no time. There is a life and a death. There are people and animals. Our thoughts exist. And the world. The universe, too. But there is no time. You might as well take it easy. Do you feel better now? I feel better. This is going to work out. Have a nice day.

I follow him with my gaze until he disappears. Then I direct my binoculars upward, past the skyscrapers, upward and upward still. To the sky. And I feel the good sensation spreading throughout my entire body.

In a sense this is enough. I can't force it much further. I have already gained more perspective than I had dared to dream about. I've seen enough. Besides, I have things to come home to. Lise. The Owl and the Pussycat phone line. The reply from Paul.

Three things.

Trees

Today is our last day in New York. I am buying a toy car for Børre. It is green and can drive across the floor if you wind it up.

Kim is going to get a book about the weather in New York, and for Lise I'm buying a pocket kaleidoscope.

It makes 24 representations of everything I look at. The most trivial things become attractive patterns. I am forced to reassess the way I see things, things that have become so commonplace that I've stopped noticing them. My brother, for example. He looks great through the kaleidoscope. Different. Lise will probably be glad when I give it to her. Presents are important. Little presents are often better than big ones. And those in between don't often amount to much.

On my way back to the apartment, I pass some workers who are cutting down old trees and bushes and planting new ones. Some pretty large trees are lying on the pavement, waiting to be put into the ground. It makes me happy to realise that somebody is thinking about trees in a metropolis like this one.

A bit further up the street, I find a fax with instructions for the workers. It says which trees and bushes are supposed to be cut down, and which ones are supposed to be planted.

The fax is lying in the street. There doesn't seem to be much use for it any more. The workers seem to know what they're doing. I pick up the fax as I walk past. My grandfather can have it. It will please him to see that somebody in New York is concerned with trees and bushes.

April 25th, 1996

Hudson St. Reconstruction Project #HWM-447W

Tree Species and Tree Count

		Spring	Fall
1. Callery Pears (Aristocrat)	40	35	5
2. Linden (Green Spire)	4	4	
3. Willow Oak	5	5	
4. Sophora (Regent)	2~~8~~	2~~3~~ 20	3
5. Ginko	5	4	1
6. Locust (Shademaster/ Honey)	28	24	4
7. Columnar Oak (Upright English)	2	2	
8. London Plane	6	4	2
9. Zelkova (Upright)	10	10	
10. Flowering Crab Apple	2	2	
~~X Hm. Lough's Count~~		~~157~~	

*Total Trees per contract =   158   ~~124~~   15

*Total Shrubs per contract =   350   (20 ? now) (73)

**Canal St. calls for 302 Shrubs, excess will be placed @ Abingdon Sq.

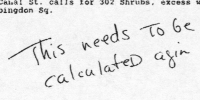

This needs To be calculated agin

ES/SS
304 Hudson/VanDam   6" CP Dead

Tree/Stump Removal Prior to Planting:

60 Hudson & Thomas St. E/S   4" Dead Ginko   OUT

N/E/C Canal & Hudson   13" London Plane (not during
                                        rush hour)

426 Hudson & St. Lukes   4" Dead Callery Pear
200 Hudson   ES   2-4" C Pr

2 Grove St. E/S   12" Remove Stump
304-310 Hudson   ES
Bleeker St. E/S betw.   2-4" CPr
W.11th to 8th Ave.
Remove the following: 13" London Plane   HPR
                                     6" London Plane   HPR
                                     4" Honey Locust   OUT
                                     4" Honey Locust   OUT

641 Hudson @ Horatio St. W/S   8" Stump

649 Hudson W/S   4" Ash

503 - 507 Hudson W/S   4" Honey Locust
507 Hudson _____ 1 CP   4" Honey Locust

ITEM # 4.16 AA -- 13
       # 4.16 AB -- 3
       # 4.16 AC -- 1

N/S BEACH ST AT TRIBECA PARK

                                    6' SJ 80%Dead REMOVE

61 JANE ST   5" AO

April 25th, 1996

Hudson St. Reconstruction Project #HWM-447W

Re: Tree Locations, Dimensions and Species

OFF-SITE, CB#1

TriBeCa Park? N/S Beach St. (remove 6" SJ)			1 Sophora
W. Broadway Beach St. to Moore St.			

1 Walker St. (Opp. 250 W. B'way)			1 Callery Pear
#250 W. B'way	W/S	Cut	1 Locust
#249 W. B'way	E/S	Cut	2 Callery Pear
#241 W. B'way	E/S	Cut	1 Zelkova
#235 W. B'way		Cut	1 Locust
N/S of White St. (relocate planter) Cut			1 Locust

#234 W. B'way	W/S	Cut	1 Sophora
#228 W. B'way	W/S	Cut	1 Callery Pear
Parking Lot	W/S		1 Callery Pear

Finn Square (@ W.B'way, Varick & Franklin)	2 Flowering Crab Apple

W. B'way: Franklin to Leonard St.

W. B'way E/S (Con-Ed)	Cut	2 Zelkova
#33 W.B'way W/S on B'way	Cut	1 Callery Pear
#33 W.B"way W/S (diner)	Cut	1 Callery Pear

Leonard St. W. B'way to Church St.

Leonard St. S/S (parking Lot)	Cut	3 Callery Pear
	Cut	3 Honey Locust

*Other: existing TP @ 348B Greenwich W/S	1 Honey locust
excavate TP @ 61 W. Greenwich	2 Sophora

EXISTING

Hudson St. Tree Location/Species
CON'T Pg.6

Charles to Perry St.
_____
#535 Hudson   (CUT 5'x 10')   1 Willow Oak
opp. 535 Hudson E/S (CUT PIT 5'x 10') 1 Linden

#541 Hudson W/S   1 Linden

NOTE (548½ Bluestone around tree,ABORIST - MUST BE PRESENT

*Careful when sidewalk work done E/S

Perry to W. 11th St.
_____
#567 Hudson W/S   (remove dead tree)   1 Callery Pear

W. 11th. St. E of Hudson
_____

N/S W. 11th (Remove sign post) Existing Pit 1 Zelkova

W. 11th. St to Bank St. (see Sht. 81 of 96)
_____
#571 Hudson W/S   1 Callery Pear

#575 Hudson W/S   1 Callery Pear

#579 Hudson W/S   1 Callery Pear

#581 Hudson W/S   1 Callery Pear
                    CUT ALL ABOVE

Bank to Bethune
_____
#585 Hudson   W/S 1 Ginko between other 2 Ginko's
    ****
    FALL MAKE NEW PIT*
    ****

Opp. #82 Bank N/S Bank (CUT SIDES of PIT) 1 Honey Locust

Hudson St. Tree Location/Species
CON'T Pg.5

#432 Hudson   E/S   1 Ginko
*1 possible @ N/S 69 Morton St. (Cut 5'x 5')   1 Sophora Locust
#436 Hudson St. S/S Morton E of Hudson   1 Locust
                                                  Locust

Morton to Barrow St.

#451 Hudson W/S   1 Willow Oak

#455 Hudson W/S   5/7 (1) Callery Pear

#460 Hudson E/S   FALL   1 Callery Pear
****
#452 Hudson E/S (Cut 5'x 10')   FALL   1 Honey Locust*
#462 Hudson E/S until Bus Stop relocated) 1 Callery Pear*
****
Barrow to Grove St.

#479 Hudson W/S (St. Lukes)   1 Sophora
                                     5/7 (1) Locust

#2 Grove St. E/S of Hudson   5/7 (2) Honey Locust
             Remove 1-12' Oak Stump

Grove to Christopher St.

#490 Hudson   E/S (PS 3)   5/7 (2) Locust

St. Luke's W/S   (just So.of Christopher)   1 Willow Oak

opp. #496 Hudson W/S (Cut Sidewalk) 5'x10' (1) Honey Locust
                                         5/7
Christopher to W. 10th St.

#254 W.10th & Hudson W/S   5/7 (1) Callery Pear
#254 W.10th.on 10th   S/S (CUT Sidewalk 5/7 (1) Callery Pear
                          5' x 10')

W. 10th St. to Charles St.

#519 Hudson   W/S   5/7 (1) Callery Pear

#524 Hudson on N/S w.10th St. (CUT 5'x 5') 1 Ginko

#532 Hudson   E/S   1 Willow Oak

Trees are one of my favourite things. Water and trees and girls.

I used to climb all day long. And often I would just sit there quietly, in a treetop. For several hours. When the foliage was thick in summer, nobody could see me. I could see everybody, but nobody could see me. I felt I was far away. And when I climbed back down, it was almost like returning home after a long journey. And I would make swings. I was dead good at making swings. I would climb up high and tie the rope to a branch. Then I'd swing. And spit. It was always fun to spit while I was swinging. If I'd been drinking milk, the saliva got nice and gooey. I'd spit incredibly long milk wads from the swing. I want to take up swinging again.

The next time I have some money, I want to go to a sports shop and buy fifty metres of climbing rope, and then I want to find a big tree, preferably right by the water, and make a swing with an enormous pendular radius, and maybe jump from the swing into the water. While Lise is watching. I look forward to that.

Now my brother is telling me to hurry up and pack. We are going home. We're flying home to Norway. I am going home to put my hammer-and-peg to the test.

As I pack the hammer-and-peg, my brother confesses to having borrowed it a couple of times while I was out. In return he wants me to admit that the trip has done me good. I admit that it has. It has done me a lot of good. I've seen a lot of things. And I have both thought and not thought.

At my best I have been completely untroubled and pleasantly thought-free. We've had a couple of frisbeeing sessions that were almost Zen. I thank my brother for it. And for the whole trip. It hasn't been cheap. My brother tells me to think nothing of it. I look well, he says. That's the important thing.

Money is not important. Money comes and goes. But brothers are important. Brothers are more important than money, my brother says.

Journey

We are on the plane. There is just sea below us. Water. I am full and sleepy. And I have a smile on my face. Something is different.

I still don't know if things fit together, or if everything will be all right in the end. But I believe that something means something. I believe in cleansing the soul through fun and games. I also believe in love. And I have several good friends, and just one bad one. And my brother is at least as friendly as I am. He's sleeping now.

I have a window seat this time. It is dark outside. But it will be light before too long. We are flying toward the light.

Now I'm drinking a sip of water, hoping that life will last. I am also hoping that Paul has written me a reply. Maybe he has told me everything. Then I can relax and let time and space be as they may.

When I get home I'm going to buy a bicycle helmet. And I want to call Lise and tell her that life is a bit like a journey, and that I am maybe, but only maybe, a really good guy.

The Reply

From: "Prof. Paul Davies" <pdavies@physics.adelaide.edu.au>
Subject: Re: writers question/time and the meaning of life (no less)
To: erlend@algonet.se (Erlend Loe)
Date: Wed, 22 May 1996 13:48:13 +0930 (CST)
Mime-Version: 1.0

Thank you for your enquiry. Since Professor Davies started receiving several
such queries per day, he has had to adopt a policy of not offering advice. I
hope you will understand.

Yours sincerely,

Heather Duff
Assistant to Paul Davies